THE KEY OF IMPASTO

Published in Canada by Engen Books, St. John's, NL.

ISBN-13: 978-1-77478-033-6

Distributed by:
Engen Books
www.engenbooks.com
submissions@engenbooks.com

First mass market paperback printing: April 2021

Cover Design: Ellen Curtis

Slipstreamers Committee:
Amanda Labonté
Ali House
AJ Ryan
Ellen Curtis
Erin Vance
Lauralana Dunne
Matthew LeDrew

THE KEY OF IMPASTO

CAROLYN R PARSONS & JD RYOT

CHAPTER ONE

"Tell me quick. You know I simply *hate* waiting."

It was rare that Professor Herbert Gamgee didn't hear someone approach him, given his lab was in a wide-open space, stark, sanitary, silver and cold that sound echoed through like an early warning alarm. Today, however, he was clueless that Cassidy Cane was behind him until she tapped him on the back and spoke. Professor Gamgee turned, and as he did, he knocked a small glass item over that rolled to the end of the table and off its edge. With the reflexes of a much younger man, he stretched out his hand and caught it before it dashed to bits on the cold hard floor. His heart pounded. *That* was a close call. He peered into the bulbous globe and gulped.

"Are you okay?" he asked.

"I'm fine, thank you. How are you doing?" Cassidy wound her hair into a ponytail and slipped a band over it to hold it in place.

"What?" Professor Gamgee asked.

"I said, I'm fine, how are you—" Cassidy repeated.

"No, not you, *her*," he said pointing to the odd-looking object he'd just saved from being bashed to dust on the floor. He turned back to it, tapped the noise-reducing headphones on his head and asked again.

"You know, Doc, there's a fine line where eccentricity slips over into wackadoodle, and you're close to crossing it. Her *who*?" Cassidy sized him up, finger at her chin. His white headphones and microphone oddly balanced with his thick glasses. Was he talking to a snow globe? No, he must have somebody on Skype. Yes. Of course.

"It was an accident, I didn't mean to...no, no, she's capable, she isn't clumsy at all. I was wearing the head-phones and I didn't...yeah maybe you're right, we can put you in a—"

"I hope you and your *snow globe* will be *very* happy to-gether. I'll leave you two alone." Cassidy lifted a sardonic brow, folded her arms and waited for him to regain his sanity. She had no intention of leaving.

"What?" He yelled, this time to Cassidy and not his imaginary friend.

"Take off the headphones." Cassidy rolled her eyes and pointed to her own ear to indicate what she was say-ing.

"What?"

"Take *off* the headphones," she repeated louder.

"Oh, yes. Cassidy. Okay, sorry, yes. Just a moment. Corie, I have to talk to Cassidy, I'll be right back," he said, before he pulled off the headphones and set them on the table.

"Who are you Skyping with?" Cassidy glanced around, looking for the computer.

"I'm not Skyping with anyone." He indicated the lap-top on a shelf, lid shut.

"Then you're talking to yourself? And what is that anyway?" She pointed to the oddly shaped rock or geode or something on his desk that he'd nearly broken when she'd startled him.

"That is not a what. It is a who. Well, it's a what as well, I guess. It's all quite spectacular really, she I mean. Both, it, and her. She's your next assignment and she's a marvel."

"She?" Cassidy moved in closer, feeling a bit ridiculous. It looked was an inanimate object. She reached out and with her fingernail. *Tap tap tap.*

"No, not that. That's her, um, container. She's inside. Look right there, at the tiny window. I didn't notice at first, either. I found this in a potato field in the Netherlands near the portal at Kleve years ago. It was filthy, I washed it and used it as a paperweight. Can you believe it's been on my desk the whole time? I thought it was an ordinary lump of glass. Forgot all about it. Until yesterday when I finally heard her."

"Okay, back up. Heard who?" Cassidy was getting exasperated at his disjointed explanation.

"Corie. Corie in the jar."

"What?"

"Look. Here. Put these on, and look."

Gamgee held out the headset and Cassidy took it. She put on the headphones, adjusting them to fit over her hair.

"Say hello," Gamgee encouraged.

"Hello," Cassidy said, shooting him a look.

"Hallo," a woman's voice answered.

"Oh, hello," Cassidy repeated. Looking around the

room for the source of the voice. "Where *is* she?"

"Look in *there*," Gamgee said with a triumphant grin. "As I said, look through the tiny window."

Cassidy bent down for a closer look at the globe. There was a tiny electronic device attached to one side with tape, otherwise, it appeared to be a ball of etched glass and not really a globe at all. It was more jar-shaped, kinda fat in the middle, flat on the bottom as if it were carved out of a solid chunk of quartz or some similar crystalline mineral. She touched the top of it again, noting it had diamond-like cuts as well, tiny facets so small that it nearly appeared to be smooth until you looked at it closely.

She picked it up.

"Careful," Gamgee cautioned.

"I'm always careful," she volleyed.

Startled that it was so lightweight, she turned it over. Hollow perhaps? It caught the light as she rotated it and colours refracted off its surface, red, yellow, blue, Primary colours only. How peculiar, she thought. Then she spotted the window Dr. Gamgee had referred to. It was tiny, no bigger than a nano sim card for a smartphone, square and clear, like a little keyhole. She squinted and peered through it.

Then it opened and she didn't need to squint anymore. Without changing at all, in any discernible way, it expanded and suddenly, somehow, there was a full-size window in front of her. An illusion of one anyway as she still held the orb in her hand. It was impossible. The scale wasn't right. She glanced away, everything appeared normal, the globe still the same size in her hand, yet when she looked at the tiny window. Bam! It grew larger so that while she held a palm-sized container, the window to the inside of it allowed her to look as though she looked out one of the windows in Professor Gamgee's lab towards the outside.

"Say hello to Corie!" Gamgee said, his voice high pitched and excited as though he were introducing her to Howard Carter, the famous archaeologist who excavated King Tut's tomb. Except this was even more unlikely than meeting a dead hero.

Cassidy looked again. She'd seen the window but no person. In fact, all she could see was a swirl of red, yellow and blue that glazed the view, like a painted curtain over a *window*. She was about to call him on his practical joke when the colours morphed into a more defined pattern and churned like a smoothie in a blender until it seemed as though all the colours in existence blended together like the molten wax of a Crayola 64 crayon pack.

Then a whorl of light arranged itself in a mesmerizing prism until a tiny dot appeared in its center. The dot, that could only be explained as a point of clarity. It grew so that the window enlarged further before her eyes and she could see into its depths.

Cassidy was held spellbound. "That's incredible," she said as fields of green grass and blue sky unfolded in her line of vision. Then, finally, into the field, walked a young woman, probably around Cassidy's age, in a blue dress with a red blouse and yellow shoes. Her hair was the colour of wheat in sunshine and a smile dented her lovely face.

"I'm Corie Kerkvest and I need you to return the key home," the pretty young girl in the globe said. "Professor

Gamgee says you are the one who can."

"I'm Cassidy Cane," Cassidy replied, breathless at the scene before her.

"Do you see her? Do you?" Professor Gamgee asked, his voice as excited as a child's.

"I do," Cassidy said. She could not tear her eyes away from the world in the palm of her hand. She didn't even want to try. She wanted to look into the depths of the orb forever.

"Oops, Corie, she's stuck, like I was. Perhaps you should—" Professor Gamgee said, noticing Cassidy's trance.

The colours faded and in a moment Corie stood under a pale blue sky as ordinary as the one outside the lab, with bland white clouds that shuffled along.

Released from the hold on her, Cassidy looked away from the globe.

She turned to Gamgee and said in her best Desi Arnaz impression, "you, professor, have some 'splaining to do."

CHAPTER TWO

"I should have thought to connect *two* amplifiers before." The professor fussed with the electronic device attached to the side of the globe next to the first one.

"Can't I just talk to her without you?" Cassidy waved to the woman inside, still reeling from it all. Corie waved back. It was so strange. She should have looked like a miniature, but some trick of the window created the illusion that the inside of this odd globe was as large as the outside world — her world. Corie, inside the strange capsule, looked to even be a few inches taller than Cassidy herself. And those colours. They were just regular colours but — not. Somehow, they enthralled her far more than regular colours ever could. She had no idea why. Perhaps it was the lighting inside that caused that peculiarity. Whatever it was, once captivated, it was impossible to look away and the joy of that beauty, the swelling of pleasure in her chest from it, well, it was inexplicable really. It made her incredibly happy yet after, left her disconcerted.

"Waiting isn't so difficult if you learn to enjoy the view," Corie said, waving her hand so that the clouds over her head turned once more from ordinary white puffs to startling red, blue and yellow swirls blending into an incandescent mix of brilliant hues.

Cassidy jumped at her voice then, once more, became mesmerized by the spectacular effects.

"Cassidy," Gamgee said.

"Leave me alone." Annoyed, she swatted the air with the back of her hand in his general direction.

"Can you both hear me? Test-test. One, two, three..."

Corie jumped and placed her hands over her ears.

"Roger," Cassidy shouted, "but it's too loud though. Turn it down. For fritter's sake, turn it down!" She had been working hard to clean up her language a bit and had taken to substituting food terms when the urge hit. Having her ears blasted by Gamgee was reason enough to break out the baked goods.

"Who is Roger?" Corie yelled, pursing her lips in confusion.

"It's a saying, it means 'yes,'" Professor Gamgee replied. This time the volume was at a normal level. He looked chuffed with himself at his cleverness at having solved their communication issue.

"Alright, now you can tell me what this is about and what the job is," Cassidy said, disappointed that the clouds were back to boring puffy white but able to look away and ask the question of the professor to his face.

"I found Corie—" Professor Gamgee said.

"I was sent outside our—" Corie said at the same moment.

"Please, stop, I can't listen to you both at once. Professor, go first. And you're still a bit loud, lower your volume a bit more please."

"Okay!" Gamgee's voice blasted. Cassidy jumped and pulled the earpieces away from her ears.

"Wrong way!"

"Oops," He adjusted something. "Sorry. Is this better?"

"Yes," Cassidy adjusted her headset as well. "Now that we're all wired and my eardrums have been saved from shattering, go on, Professor." She peered at Corie who still had hands over her ears, just in case.

"I found Corie, the container specifically, in a potato field in Holland when I was scouting the portal there. It was covered in filth and I tossed it in my bag with a few other items. I brought it back with me and shined it up, laid it on my desk and pretty much forgot about it.

"Until I finally attentioned him," Corie said.

"How long has it been here?"

"A year," Gamgee responded. "Just a bit over that really. Anyway, I thought nothing of it. It sat there pretty and useful as a paperweight."

Cassidy had noticed it on his desk; hadn't thought much of it either. He had an assortment of odd artifacts about, some of which she'd acquired for him in her many jaunts through the portals this past while.

"I tried so hard to call him. To wake up him. But little is the sound of me." Corie had an interesting voice pattern but Cassidy could understand her. That would improve as the universal translating kicked in.

"So, you sat here? You could hear him? Us? But couldn't get us to respond?"

"Yes. Sound it is in but not it is out. Certainly, it was not much to listen until arrived you. Professor talks no interesting things. All sciency and boring it is."

"Physics isn't for everyone." Gamgee bristled and looked put out.

Cassidy held back a grin. He was as dry as paper at times though no one dared tell him that.

"I learn the language of you but no you me hear. And I try not until you much understood. Then I hear you, Traveller! That made me harder try."

"You found a way to be loud enough for him to hear you?"

"I found a way for him to see me. By making my, bows of rain."

"She means rainbows."

"I understood her."

Corie had learned the English language very well by listening and while she flipped words around sometimes, she was easy to understand because her pronunciation was nearly perfect. Oddly, Cassidy's translation abilities hadn't kicked in and while translating a new dialect of English into correct English was a bit of a challenge, it didn't matter. She could understand her perfectly well.

"Now we have to get her back home and the key has to be returned," Gamgee said. His spectacles perched on the bridge of his nose, his owlish eyes darting between the globe and Cassidy as he spoke.

"So, this receptacle that you're in, isn't your home?" Cassidy asked.

"Oh, no, this was my pod of escape. Created by my friend to save me. But I can't live here longer. I have to go back home."

"You see, she's the rightful Queen of her people," the

professor explained.

"President, but only *to be*, no *is*." Corie corrected. "We are democratic. I was voted. It was a large majority."

"She's the president-elect," Gamgee corrected. "She was in dire danger it seems and her friend, Eryn, figured out how to save her. By putting her in the pod and throwing her out the portal.

"Why the pod? Why not just come here. Or were you afraid because you are so tiny?"

"Because we know not if my form can live in your world without. But also, I am not tiny. I am the size of you. The pod smallerizes. But in my world, we'd be like-sized."

"What? So you've been shrunk?"

"It is hard. The inside of here is big, the outside of here is small. I am big inside. My container is small outside."

"Like a TARDIS?" Cassidy's eyes grew round.

"Without the time thing," Gamgee said. "At least, I think. Don't know for sure. If there are portals, and *smallerization* perhaps there are temporal possibilities as well." He grabbed a pencil and paper and started jotting down numbers and formulas. "Who's to say if there isn't a difference in time between our world and hers? We cannot know these things without further studies and the mathematics of it all is boggling even to me, and if I start figuring and I—"

"See, he is not exciting with the words," Corie said, rolling her eyes.

"Right, so, anyway, let's get back on topic." Cassidy's grin broke through, at Gamgee's crestfallen expression.

"So, if you're not sure you can survive in my world,

how can you know if I can live in yours?"

"Because travellers have come to our world before. The atmosphere is surviving okay but the militia no."

"So the air won't kill me but your army will. So why won't it work the opposite way?"

"A thousand days ago when it was old times, the old Gaughan-president make it so. I don't know how she did that."

"A thousand days?"

"See! There is a time thing. I think their time is different than ours. First I thought it was a language thing, but it seems their days are very long. Either way, this previous Gaughan made it so their people can't survive out here. Even though we can in their world." Professor Gamgee was still jotting notes down, focused again on the time element.

"That would explain why a year doesn't feel long to her." Cassidy guessed.

"That and because beautiful it is in the small world," Corie replied, waving her hand around and suddenly grass sprung up around her feet in more shades of green than stars in the night sky, waving and dancing about on the ground and into the distance. Cassidy lost herself in the beauty of it until it faded and Corie regained her attention by waving it all away.

"I can't think of anything else when you do that," Cassidy said. "I can't stop looking. Is your entire world like that? Because if it is, I will be absolutely useless. Professor, does it suck you in too? So that you forget everything else?"

"Yes. And you're right, there is no way you could navigate her world with such a distraction. In the globe she can change things but not in her world. Travellers have been there before, as she said, but they never get past the guards. I think that's why the Gaughan easily removed anyone who entered her world. These other travellers didn't know what it was like there and weren't prepared to handle their preoccupation with the colours."

"So if I do this, how do you expect me to not become mesmerized and captured immediately?"

"Because the fix is easy, it turns out. I tried a few things before you got here." He handed Cassidy a pair of aviator-style amber sunglasses. Ordinary, black-framed cheapies, not even Ray Bans. She put them on. The professor put a pair over his bottle-thick specs and then they peered together into the tiny window that somehow drew their vision forward so that they could both see in.

"Do your magic," Professor Gamgee requested.

Corie waved her hands and once more the brilliant green grass grew around her feet and the clouds in the sky burst into myriad colours. The air morphed into a dark blue and across the backdrop, a million stars swirled into being in a glorious yellow and orange pattern. Flowers sprung up from between the blades of verdant grass and waved their haughty yellow heads in an invisible wind. All this happened with all the glorious splendour as it had before, but this time Cassidy could think and look away, smile and respond. She was enamoured but not as literally spellbound as she was previously.

"That's spectacular but now I only see it, I don't feel like it has a hold on me. Much better." She pushed the sunglasses up.

"I wonder if maybe we can use a Bluetooth earpiece instead of these big headphones?" Cassidy asked. "I can hide that, blend in better?"

"Yes, we'll modify this. I had to amplify her voice to hear her well and made do but, certainly, I think we can make a smaller, wireless gadget before you go. To communicate I quickly modified a digital hearing-aid and connected it to the headset. All very simple really, but I was in a rush." Gamgee said. "We'll improve it a great deal before you leave."

"Now. Let's clarify a few things." Cassidy pushed the Ambervision glasses up and looked straight at Corie. "You were elected president of your country but your enemies decided to stop you so a friend threw you out here in a pod to save you but now you want me to go back to a place where others like me normally can't last more than a few moments before being tossed out and my only protection is a pair of cheap Ambervision sunglasses where we communicate via a device made from a hearing aid and a Bluetooth earpiece?"

"Well, yes…" Corie admitted.

"And your excellent navigation skills," Gamgee added.

"And if they catch you with me, they may not simply toss you out, they may imprison you. I am their president-elect who has vanished."

"What are the other obstacles?"

"They will be guarding the portal and the Crystal House of government. The service will not allow constituents into the Crystal House. I'm afraid that is a big challenge."

"Given there was an attempt on your life, why do you think it's safe for you now?"

"I don't. But I was only supposed to be hidden, not exiled. I must go back because people need democratic president, not stolen one."

Cassidy removed the amber glasses, Corie wiped a hand around so that the swirling mesmerizing colours vanished, much to her disappointment.

"I see." Cassidy folded her arms across her chest and pondered.

"Professor, what do you think?"

"I think it's likely a very dangerous trip. That you will need to utilize skills you've never used before and that it might be one from which you never return," Gamgee said.

A ripple of fear zipped down Cassidy's spine. So much could go wrong. This journey to Corie's land sounded rife with danger and was likely a journey of pure folly that could wind up with her imprisonment or worse. Plus, she hated the idea of a companion on an excursion such as this one. She had always been a loner on her adventures and sometimes she'd come close to disaster. Corie would be a distraction. So much of her success depended on instinct. This was a bad idea.

She looked from Corie to Professor Gamgee, all these thoughts swirling in her head like the magic in the domed container Corie inhabited.

"Perfect," she said. "Let's do it!"

CHAPTER THREE

It was not tulip season so Zundert, Holland didn't have the brilliant tulip fields The Netherlands was famous for. Cassidy would have to return in March or April and tour around Lisse a couple of hours south of this municipality if she wanted to enjoy their brilliant display. The famous windmills didn't have a specific season however, and near a potato farm behind the stone house of a local farmer was just such a structure, De Riekermolen, originally built in 1636.

"These are dreamt of in our land too," Corie's voice came through the tiny Bluetooth speaker in Cassidy's ear. They'd placed the orb in an exterior pocket of the backpack strapped to Cassidy with a small clear plastic front so she could see out her window.

"They are? So did you choose not to build them?"

"Of course we built them. If we dream something beautiful, it is built." Corie said as though that should be obvious.

"Ah, yes but here we have a few more steps that we take between thought and getting something built. Some ideas are not so good. These are though. Windmills were very useful. I think we're close to the portal. We're clear on the plan, right? We enter and you guide me past the guards. I'll be faster than most because I won't be distracted by the scenery like all the others and should make it to the Alizaron Hills where we'll solidify our plans before we journey to the presidential residence. Some changes may have occurred since you left that you're unaware of. But does that sound right?"

"Yes," Corie replied. "Where we get Eryn, start a search for the key, if he hasn't found it, and then reclaim my right to be president."

"And the militia?"

"Will follow the one with the key."

"And Eryn? You're sure he'll be willing to help?"

"Yes, he is trustful worth. Do you see a field of potatoes?"

"Potato field right over there, creek running through it past the windmill, so we're close."

"I wish I could guide you more," Corie said, "but being tossed through like a ball in a game is not memory making. And then I couldn't see until Gamgee cleaned my window."

"I hear it!" Cassidy said. A slight whirring sound indicated she should turn. She sniffed the air and veered to the left.

"It is a sound? Wait. Is it a smell too? My memory of it is of something lovely like—"

"Absinthe? I smell absinthe, licorice and spice." Cassidy sniffed again, turning towards where the aroma was stronger.

"Our word is turpenia, and yes, it is a delicious beverage. As your world loves its wine, we adore our turpinia. I recall a strong smell of that now. I had forgotten! Unfortunately, like your wine, a little accentuates the beauty of our lives but too much causes a blur of our colours and erases the light from it. We do not overindulge. For me to smell it so, it is too much." She broke into a sob.

"Okay, pull yourself together. You're a president and we're on a mission. No time for tears. Let's go." Corie sniffed again as Cassidy walked along the creek, following her nose towards the strong odor. She plodded past a wind-row of trees, walking like a tightrope walker between the lines of knee high potatoes, going straight through for acres. The ground became muddier and wetter as she walked and the smell of the heady fragrance grew in its intensity. The stench of the absinthe overpowered her as she closed in. She wrinkled her nose, her stomach rumbled, rejecting what had become a foul odour. As the colours had through Corie's window, the odour of the pungent elixir was entirely overwhelming. Cassidy took the bright red scarf off her neck and tied it over her face.

"This stinks," she grumbled into the Bluetooth.

"It smells like too much," Corie agreed, although for her it was somewhat dulled by the protection of her container.

Cassidy plodded on a few more steps then stopped. The suction of the mud held her fast.

"What the...?" She tried lifting her boots but to no avail.

"Is there a problem?"

"I'm stuck, Corie, I can't move even an inch." She wrenched to one side then the other trying to twist her boots out of the gluey mud. "I don't know what to do—"

Boom! The earth gave way and was drawn down, down, down, further, further, and further into the muck until she was up to her waist. She looked around for something to grab as she sank deeper and deeper into what smelled like pure absinthe, the essence of fennel and wormwood assaulting her nostrils as the ground pulled her in.

And then she saw the portal. Right at that moment that she stopped sinking. Of course, she thought. The mudhole was in the perfect spot to deter anyone from approaching it, if the heady stink didn't send them back first. Invisible a moment prior, now Cassidy could see it clearly.

Like a glazed window, the air swirled a slightly different colour, and someone in a panic, not looking for the opening, would be too distracted to see it or care. They'd haul themselves out of the mud at this point and go home to clean up. She had stopped sinking and could move again.

She used her arms to create purchase and hauled herself towards the portal, the smell of absinthe strong but bearable as she moved forward. Then with a big slurp she was out and only a few feet from the portal.

"I better get sorted first, Corie." She sat on the grass and whipped off her boots, dumping the gooey mud out, grimacing as the smell of the absinthe lingered around in the air. She quickly put her damp boots back on and stood, closing in on the portal that was now like a swirling frosted window as though a stained-glass pane had been caught in a whirlpool, all the colours swirling and glittering against the backdrop of the sky.

"Corie, I see it. Are you ready?" Her heart skipped a little and her stomach did a familiar flip-flop that could have been fear but was equally likely to be excitement. Or like the portal, a blend of all feelings one has when one is about to leap into the unknown.

"I am very ready," Corie said, excited to be going home at last.

Cassidy stood, bright green pants, now splattered with mud, blue top in the latest fashion Corie recalled from her home dimension, and a huge grin on her face. She pushed up the black-framed aviator glasses and steeled herself for the adventure, a rush of adrenaline bringing a smile to her face as she leapt.

"Ouch," Cassidy said, landing faster than she expected, a pain shooting up her leg. A curse word would have followed but before it could escape her lips she was struck from behind and knocked to her knees. She knew a second blow would follow so she ducked, then dodged to the right. The guard missed and she ducked to the left as he yelled for back up. Cassidy righted herself, noted there was no real pain in her wrenched foot and got her bearings fast. She sized up the guard, a portly old fellow with nothing more than a club type weapon. She could outrun him even if her ankle had been injured.

The distraction of the colours didn't require good guards at the portal and Cassidy had not been surprised that she evaded this guy's slow reflexes. Two more guards were running — if you could call it that — both of them, a man and woman, so languid in their movements they could have been a slow-motion film scene.

"Are they *all* this slow?" She yelled into the microphone. Without waiting for a response, she broke into a run.

"Yes, we put older, retired guards here. It's an easy job. Go, keep right, always keep right," Corie's voice in her ear said.

"Right, got it," Cassidy's swift legs darted towards the most brilliant green forest she had ever seen.

"Go, you are faster, I know you are." Corie encouraged. Cassidy didn't answer. But her speed increased at the pep talk in her ear. The distance between her and the guards lengthened.

"You are the fastest runner in my world," Corie said, and Cassidy believed her as even more distance fell between them. A glance back over her shoulder indicated that she was even further ahead, and she marveled how she had run so far, so fast. A handful of other guards had joined the first, but they had all stopped, watching as Cassidy disappeared into the spectacular forest.

Winded from the run, Cassidy found a tree and sat beneath it. She inhaled slowly. She'd run faster than necessary really, but better too fast than too slow.

Cassidy looked around at the spectacular colours. "How is it that things are so much *more* here?" She hoisted the backpack off her shoulder, opened the pouch and lifted Corie out. She peered inside. Like it had in her own dimension, the window gave the impression that the interior of the canister was so much bigger than it could possibly be.

"I suppose we are good at being more when more is good. And the opposite is true as well. We can be less when less is good. It was more of the less that got me inside a small place."

"Uh?" Cassidy rolled her eyes. "I think you're saying that you are able to create a small space that looks like *more* inside." Cassidy swiped at the mud on the lower half of her limbs, the smell of absinthe fading now that they were inside. The *how* of this all was a mystery. She mulled things over in her mind. Corie was president-elect and there was a key somewhere that they had to find and deliver to her ally, Eryn, and somehow this time Corie would be staying and standing up for her presidency instead of hiding in a jar and allowing herself to be tossed into another dimension. How this would happen, Cassidy didn't know. She'd placed a lot of trust in a tiny woman in a snow globe.

The best thing she could do was take stock of where things were right at the moment. She looked around her.

The damp moss huddled against the trees smelled of fragrant greenness while the dark fertile earth perfumed the ground upon which she sat. Ferns waved in a warm breeze that flitted through the spaces between the large evergreens and tall deciduous trees, that bore a remarkable resemblance to a regular forest back home. The woodland sounds were similar as well, and Cassidy identified several familiar chirps. With the glasses on, there were many similarities between their two places. The intensity of colour and light being the only difference and even with her eyes shaded by the amber lensed glasses, it was far brighter here and somehow, *extra*.

"This smells so much like home, like a regular forest," she commented.

"Then a regular forest is as good as smells become,"

Corie said.

"So, do you still want to stay inside? Perhaps we can make our way back together? Or do we stick to the plan?"

"I must stay inside. I need an apparatus to come outside. But even if I could, should somebody see me too soon we may not get inside the presidential house and that is where I need to be. I will have to stay inside, though I long to be free now that I'm home. Plus, I have to be on the pedestal." Corie wiped at a tear and Cassidy glanced away.

"An apparatus? A pedestal? Alright, we'll discuss these details later." Their flight had been booked so quickly and between cab drivers and other passengers they hadn't had a moment alone to discuss the details.

Cassidy unzipped the backpack, pulled out a smaller pack that had been custom made. For jumping through the portal the backpack was more secure. but for regular traversing of this world, Cassidy would transfer her into the front. The pocket they'd created was shaped perfectly for the canister that held Corie. She slipped it in, wriggling it to get it to the bottom. Then she aligned the window through the tiny square at the front of it so Corie could see out. Once that was in place, she slipped the straps over her shoulders, winding them around and buckling the bottom ends like a belt.

"Alright in there?" She knew Corie was, of course. Whoever had designed this weird pod had made it so Corie didn't bounce around in it at all no matter what sort of shaking happened. Cassidy pulled her ponytail tight, stood and threw her backpack over her shoulders again. Corie simply stood at the window and watched nearly completely unaffected by all the movement.

"I am well, and this is better so much." She exclaimed.

"It is for me too. You can give me better direction. So
where to now, President Corie?"

"To the mountains! Go straight forward, the path will
be there."

"To the mountains!" Cassidy repeated and started
her trek forward towards the tall peaks that prodded the
clouds in the distance.

CHAPTER FOUR

It took an hour to walk the scenic path into the Mountains of Senremy. Cassidy walked along the path, until they finally came to a plateau. There, a large village, Nommickdamen, sat underneath the foothills of a massive mountain range that stretched far into the lavender clouds and extended beyond their line of vision in either direction.

The town itself sat on an ocean inlet that travelled miles inland and around which wooden houses, brightly painted in all imaginable colours had been built. Like jellybeans they perched bright and joyful at the edge of the bay. The porches and walkways were adorned with brilliant blooms of unfamiliar flowers, their blossoms wafting a heady scent in the temperate air. The architecture of the homes had a European flair similar to Amsterdam but with an almost cartoonish extravagance to them. The sun blazed hot over the village and Cassidy felt a trickle of sweat down her spine. She whipped off her backpack, pulled out a canteen, wiped her brow and took a big swig. The cool water was like nectar and she took a second before replacing the lid.

"This is the land of *Moreisbetter*," she mused to Corie before replacing her backpack. The mud had dried and she could dust it off her legs now and even her boots were dryer as they strolled along the meadow to a wooden boardwalk that skirted the bright blue inlet. Fishmongers held out samples of their catch as other boats made off into the horizon, their vivid red, blue and yellow planking and sails blooming bright against the cornflower blue sky.

Cassidy blended in well. Aside from everybody wearing primary colours exclusively, they could have been home. She strolled through a small marketplace, pretending to browse.

"We need a car, or some other sort of transportation," Cassidy mused.

"There should be some around here somewhere."

"Do you see one?" Cassidy asked after they'd walked for another fifteen minutes.

"Keep walking. There should be a car park near the red house at the end."

"This street is so long I didn't think it had an end," Cassidy said.

"There, see?"

"Those are not cars! Those are electric scooters!"

"Is it? I mix the words up then."

"Maybe you should speak your language, what is it? Danch? Let me just use universal interpretation instead of using English," Cassidy said. She could drive a scooter, these looked similar to regular old earth scooters overall so that wasn't a problem. They'd just be more exposed than they would be in a car. And significantly less comfortable.

"Yes, I could do that. I will speak Danch," she said in her native language. Immediately Cassidy went into interpretation mode, the lilting dialect of English Corie had been speaking vanishing in an instant.

"Wow, that is much better. Who knew?"

"Is my English that bad?"

"No, it's actually quite excellent but the translation is superior it seems. We really don't need miscommunication to cause us problems. Now which one?" Cassidy walked along the rows of scooters so that Corie could see the choices."

The blue scooter with the red seat. That one. It belongs to the fishmonger and he won't miss it until later."

"How do you know it's his?"

"It's on his licence plate," Corie replied. Cassidy autotranslated the licence plate. Sure enough, it said "Purveyor of Sea Catch."

"So, I just steal a scooter?"

"*Borrow* a scooter." Corey corrected. "We shall replace it."

Cassidy glanced around the busy parking area. "So nobody will notice if I take it?"

"Nobody ever takes anything here, so they'll assume you own it."

"So I'm your first thief?"

"No, we borrow here. As I said, nobody steals, they borrow and repay."

"That's a lot of trust. And isn't he going to be inconvenienced when he discovers it missing?

"Why would he be inconvenienced? Somebody will

lend him another. He will know his will be returned or replaced."

"Your people are very trusting."

"My people are mostly very trustworthy."

"But not all or we wouldn't be here."

"Sadly yes. Not all." Corie's voice held despair at her betrayal.

"Well, cheer up, we'll get things all fixed up for you. Hang on, President-elect! Here we go." Cassidy heaved a leg over the seat of the scooter and settled in. She glanced around. Nobody looked their way.

"Hold the brake on the left handle, then push the yellow button."

Cassidy did and the scooter purred to life. She checked out the instrument panel, sized up the handlebars.

"You just push the initiator," Corie said. It's the handle on the right. That will make it go forward, again to go faster and then again to go even faster. I would only do the first and second notches until you have practiced a bit."

"Okay. No helmet?" Cassidy didn't fancy a fractured scull in a strange new world. Or even in the old one.

"Oh, yes, in the pouch beside the seat."

"There is a little pouch here, but that can't be it." Cassidy looked on the other side.

"It will be blue with a helmet symbol on it."

Cassidy bit her lip and narrowed her eyes. This tiny pouch, the size of a coffee mug could not possibly hold a helmet, but she opened it anyway. Inside was a small, flat, silver square. She reached in and pulled it out.

"Unfold it." Corie instructed.

A doubtful expression on her face, Cassidy did as she was told, pulling apart the tiny foil square. It opened into a hat shape that somewhat did resemble a helmet.

"This? This is soft. How does this protect the head from injury?" She slipped it over her hair.

"Fasten it." Corie grinned. She liked surprising Cassidy and anticipated this would be a good one.

Cassidy pulled the band underneath her chin and with a snap connected it to the other side. The moment she did the soft silver material engaged in a metamorphosis whereby it became a solid helmet, perfectly molded and held fast to Cassidy's head.

"This is spectacular," Cassidy said, moving her head from side to side. "How the heck does that happen?" She closed up the case, considered its size, touched the helmet and again shook her head.

"More is less when less is needed," Corie's voice in her ear said.

"And less is more when more is needed. I don't think this is possible. How?"

"How it works is a secret. It uses proprietary technology owned by the government. It must only be used for the betterment of the people."

"And using it to save the president-elect counts for sure, right?"

"Eryn thought it counted. It's the first time it was used to secure a person, however."

"Wasn't that risky?"

"I've never been opposed to some risk. You can't rise to become president without taking chances."

"A girl after my own heart. Well, now we're off to the

castle."

"Presidential residence," Corie corrected.

"Presidential residence. Got it. Hang on."

"I can't really hang on?" Corie's wan voice said.

"I mean, here we go!" Cassidy said and hit the control. The scooter started to move. She felt for her balance, settled into her seat. Slowly they inched forward. Feeling the familiarity of the machine — it was not unlike a scooter back home — feet on the pedals she pulled out, checking each way for traffic before edging out onto the quiet street then around and up over the hill and away from the canal side of the village.

She hit the control again, picking up speed. She tested the brakes. They lurched to a stop. Too much. She moved forward again, this time using a gentle touch on the brake control easing to a stop.

This street was filled with traffic, and more people felt better to Cassidy, less out in the open and noticeable, a preferred state on a stolen vehicle.

"Follow this upwards then you will come to the sign for Senremy Road. That is the mountain road that will take you through to Dream Tams, the capital city of Ashlen Der Tenth where the presidential residence awaits."

CHAPTER FIVE

Senremy Road. Dream Tams. Ashlen Der Tenth. Cassidy repeated the three over and over under her breath so she wouldn't forget. *Senremy Road. Dream Tams. Ashlen Der Tenth.*

Cassidy laid on the speed once she was out of traffic and in the clear on the isolated mountain pass. Without the rumble of a noisy engine and the incredibly smooth handling of the scooter, she found she was enjoying herself immensely. The mountains were unlike any others she had ever seen. The rock formations were an azure colour in some places and then further along the road was tunnelled between cliffs of the brightest emerald green. The trees were taller in the foothills. As she ascended, she found open places where the mountainside shielded her with a rock side on the left and a clear open drop on her right that was filled with trees of amber, gold, red, and green. The sky above was a deep blue and the roadside was edged with blossoms in every possible shade of yellow. There was little black or white visible although there must have been to create the dark purples of the landscape in the distance and ruddy brown of the dirt road. It was highly distracting in its stark bold beauty, even with the sunglasses. So much so that the other scooters were nearly at her taillights before she saw them in the tiny rear-view mirror on her right handlebar.

"Corie, we've got company. Bright fuchsia scooters with white lights flashing. Police?"

"Yes, law keepers. Are you going too fast?"

"What is the speed limit?"

"Second button!"

"I'm on button four, butter on a biscuit!" Cassidy exclaimed, shooting a glance at the mirror.

"Hit button five! If they catch us, they will put us inside the dungeon for this. We can't delay, we must get away."

"Alright, hang on tight!" Cassidy flicked the accelerator to five and the whirring of the scooter's purr got a shade higher. The wind slapped around her face and she saw a distance between her and the law enforcement behind her grow incrementally in the tiny mirror. Revved from the excitement of the chase she leaned into the wind and considered the road before her. It was narrow with a thousand-foot drop on one side, a steep rockface on the other, turns and twists like spaghetti in a bowl, and nowhere to go but up. With the cops of another realm hot on her trail, a tribble of excitement flitted through her. Now *this* was an adventure.

The cops narrowed the gap again and Cassidy considered the button. She felt like she was flying now, and the quietness of this scooter's engine amplified that feeling. This was a new vehicle to her and these were treacherous mountain roads. She wasn't afraid of heights, but she had no desire to die by falling from a great one into a forest, no matter how leafin' pretty it was. She leaned in further, kept going forward but the police were gaining on her.

Then she spotted an approaching scooter. It appeared to have the same markings as those at her tail. Cinnamon Buns, she thought. Still, kept going, the momentum driving her forward, pure adrenaline in her veins now.

They could stop her, but would they? Suddenly the cops ahead of her stopped. They maneuvered their bikes sideways to create a roadblock. They knew she'd have to stop or slam into them. She slowed a little to give herself a second or two to think.

Then bam, the bike accelerated at a push of the button. And they were back up to six.

"Hang on Corie, your cops are playing chicken and I'm not one. We're going through."

"Yes! That is the right thinking! You are the best scooter rider on this mountain, I know you can go through and past them at your top speed. You are so much better than they are."

"I believe you!" Cassidy shouted and with a loud whoop she pushed the final button igniting a flame beneath the bike that shot it upwards and forwards at the same time. It rose only a few feet off the ground, but it was enough to take Cassidy up, up, up, then over, over, over the police scooters and onwards along the mountain trail until they were well past any chance of the police gaining on them, then she pulled her scooter back to six level, applied the brake a touch and they slowed and lowered until the wheels touched down on solid ground. Upon impact Cassidy lost control of the scooter for a moment, bouncing like a rubber ball but she regained it by leaning in the opposite direction, eyes firmly on the road. Once she was on solid ground she decreased further to a far more sensible three speed.

"Woah, these things can fly!" Cassidy said with a loud laugh of delight.

"All the things can fly if you write them so, I knew it." Corie said. "But today it was just this scooter."

"Did you know it could?"

"The first flying thing I saw was in your world. Once I believed it could, as you did, so it could."

"This is a very strange place, Corie. But I like it."

"I do as well, Cassidy Cane. It is good to be home."

CHAPTER SIX

Stars popped out in spiral clusters against a darkened blue sky. Cassidy manoeuvred the scooter up a pathway towards a bright yellow cottage trimmed with yellow. Corie directed her to a doorway on the side and they parked with the scooter facing out the path in case a getaway was required.

"We'll rest here for the night. This is The Lamartine Cottage" Corie said. "It once belonged to our greatest artist. I purchased it after I graduated from Huysmans School of the Arts." Corie knew she could sleep at any time, but Cassidy wasn't in a controlled pod and needed to rest before entering the city tomorrow.

Cassidy looked around the cottage. It was essentially one large room with a kitchen to the left and on the right there was a bed facing a wall of windows. Everything in the room was painted various shades of white giving it a sense of space in the small surroundings. It was a stark contrast to the brilliant colours of the outside world which could still be seen, despite it being dark outside, through the large panes of glass that overlooked the natural environment.

"This view is spectacular." Cassidy walked over to the window. Outside a lake glittered in the light of a fat gibbous moon. Surrounded by forest, she felt calm and relaxed for the first time since entering Corie's world.

"I agree. And you can remove the glasses. The night will protect you from the enthrallment."

Cassidy slipped off the amber visions. The view outside the window transformed from a darkened pretty scene to a swirling canvas of colour against a backdrop of brilliant flaming stars. Cassidy was spellbound. But not literally this time.

"It's like I can see the wind," she said. She pulled off the pouch that carried Corie's container and set it on a table by the bed facing the same view that mesmerized her.

"You can. But you can also look away at night. It's not as magnetic."

"Yes. Perhaps we should have come at night. Just travelled through and I wouldn't have needed the glasses."

"I didn't know the time difference between your space and mine," Corie said. "We got lucky. Our night lasts eight hours only. We will have lots of daylight to finish this journey."

Cassidy rarely knew what she was getting into when she entered a new dimension, and this was the first time she had a guide. It would be highly unfair to expect her to know how to make this one hundred percent easier. But it certainly helped. Almost too much.

"I feel like this is too easy," Cassidy said, pulling out a toothbrush. When had she had time before to enjoy such luxury on a mission?

"That chase by the law enforcers was easy?"

Cassidy grinned. "No, that was, er, somewhat challenging."

"Then what is easy?"

"Perhaps it's this." Cassidy waved her arm around the cottage. "It feels very cozy and safe. It's also beautiful."

"Thank you. I like it too. It's a retreat really. A place to meet my muse."

"And this muse is very important to you?"

"Ah, yes. Inspiration is everything. Imagination is our most glorious gift, and we must allow it free reign to fully develop our society."

Cassidy waved her toothbrush around, "Hold that thought," she said as she went into the bathroom, brushed her teeth, and slipped into the shower, scrubbing off the mud still caked on her from earlier in the day. She returned in a sheath of white that Corie said would be hanging in the bathroom. Everything inside white, everything outside all the colours possible.

"All sorted?" Corie asked.

When Cassidy glanced inside the pod, she saw that Corie was dressed in white nightwear similar to what she'd given Cassidy.

"I have questions. Are you too tired?" Cassidy asked.

"No, it's been an easy day for me. Please ask what you want to know."

"Explain your politics. How you get elected. Who runs?"

"Oh, that is a very interesting thing. Mainly we have a competition as to who can do the most for people's lives. Everybody gets a vote, man, woman, and child and voting is mandatory."

"Children vote too?"

"Of course, even children, though parents may help them understand but who better to have new ideas and great understanding of what can be, the potential out in life, than those at the start of it?"

"I guess. And whoever gets the most votes wins?"

"Yes."

"You won?"

"By what you would call a landslide. My imagination is far superior to my opponent's."

"Your imagination? What about your policies."

"Well, they are built accordingly, after I'm elected."

Cassidy's look of disbelief was not subtle.

"Surely that's not far-fetched. Your world has similar."

"No, we don't."

"Do you think your amazing airplanes exist without somebody imagining flying? Radio? Have you ever seen a radio wave? Still, you have radio, wireless internet, electricity. You had people on your moon?" Corie replied. "We have no flying. We have no birds so we have not thought of it."

"Wow, no flying? Also, those people are not who we elect to run our countries."

"Perhaps they should be. The people with the best imaginations for what could be, the dreamers should lead those who implement the ideas, which in turn leads to better society."

"But there is a reality that to be good at governing you need to be more business-like, more pragmatic."

"We take a different approach. We elevate the creators,

the visionaries and put them in places of leadership. The artists, the poets, music makers. The storytellers imagine and share the world we want to live in. Then the scientists, the businesses, all work to ensure it is realized."

"Is everything you think of eventually created?"

"Of course not. We have many failures. But that isn't a worry. We're looking for innovative thoughts and new, outrageous ideas in our leaders. We elect dreamers and thinkers and worry not about the impossibility."

"What about the economy?"

"It follows that if you're imagining, researching, developing and building you're also selling." She lifted her shoulders in a shrug as if to say, *this is not rocket science*.

"Taxes?"

"Very unpopular. But necessary."

"It sounds perfect."

"It is not. I wouldn't have been exiled to your world if it were. My campaign was good. I wrote the story with all of my imagination of flying into space and going as far as we could go. I performed a play with all the joy and hope, fears and laughter of the human experience and I sang a song of love and heartbreak, healing, faith and family. Then I painted our world in its exquisite beauty so that people loved it more and cared more for it. This is all we do to campaign, and I told the biggest and best dreams, so I won."

"So, nothing about policy or taxes. The economy?"

"If people know to imagine the impossible, all the facets of the human reality, all the rewards of a life of love, and know their world is so beautiful they would not harm it for anything but rather bask in its health, then they will pay exactly the taxes required, find the right policies and politics and science to create all they need to be happy citizens, will they not? Everything starts with what you imagine. You would call this inspiration, and for you, it is separate from politics. For us, that is the foundation. We call it, navgoh or truelife."

"What was this big idea that you had, that got you elected and tossed out into our realm?"

"It wasn't any of my big ideas. It was a smaller, much more practical one. I wanted to use these globes, like the one I'm in, for our prisoners. Give them quality of life even while isolated. Right now, they are in cages and dungeons. This technology was dreamt of by my predecessor, built by his team and launched shortly before he retired. I wanted to utilize it further and make more humane prisons out of them. To give people worlds to live in that were interesting and healing for them."

"Wow! That's advanced thinking. I would think it a big idea."

"Perhaps, though we already feel that people who do wrong aren't necessarily unable to contribute. And they are still people. So perhaps it's a bigger step in your world to this idea, than to ours."

"And who decided this wasn't a good idea?"

"The people who own the prisons, naturally," Corie said.

"Naturally." Cassidy rolled her eyes. Not so very different after all, she thought. "So, this place isn't perfect?"

"Nothing is perfect, and that's never the dream we imagine. People will always get sick, have heartbreak, do wrong, be wronged and feel all the things people feel.

They will give birth, and die, and in between there will be problems. If that changed there'd be no more need for imagination and creativity would there?"

"Do you think it is possible that your friend, Eryn, threw you into our world to save you? Or to be rid of you?" The question had been on Cassidy's mind since their first meeting and asking it was imperative. If Eryn were not the hero Corie thought he was, then she needed to know.

"Eryn is the person who got me elected. He was also in line to govern with me as deputy president. I think he is trustworthy."

"Think, but not certain?"

"Nothing is certain."

"I guess we have no choice but to trust that then, until we know better." Cassidy slipped under the covers of the bed, fluffed up a pillow and yawned. "I'm gonna get a bit of shut-eye. Good night, Corie."

"That is true. Sleep well, Cassidy Cane," Corie said.

"I'll try. I don't know if I've ever slept well on a mission."

"You will sleep better than you have ever slept before, for eight hours at least," Corie suggested from her spot on the table.

And interestingly enough Cassidy awoke, exactly eight hours later, as rested as she'd ever been in her life.

CHAPTER SEVEN

And it was good she was well rested and in peak form because peering through the window into the cottage was a tall man with long wild red hair who appeared as though he was ready to break through the glass and kill her.

Cassidy leapt from the bed and reached over, fumbling for the earpiece. She jammed it in her ear, never taking her eyes off him.

He waved.

"Corie, there is a man. Do you see him."

"Of course I do. He is the caretaker of my cabin. His name is Galon. He is harmless."

"He doesn't look harmless!"

"He just isn't expecting you to be here. You must go and invite him in. Don't tell him I'm here."

"What will I say? How will I explain my presence?"

"You're smart, Cassidy Cane. But I'll help. Put on your sunglasses. The light—" She was right, the sun was starting to brighten out beyond the caretaker's back and Cassidy reached over and put the black-framed lenses on her face.

Grabbing a robe as Corie directed her to, she walked

over to the door.

"Galon?" She queried, repeating the name Corie said.

"Yes, but who are you?" He scratched his head, his expression still somewhat murderous.

"I'm a friend of Corie, she told me to use this cottage any time I travel through the area. And yes, while I know my friend has disappeared, I had hoped the cottage would still be available for my use and here it was, vacant. So, I stopped for the night. My apologies."

"Yes, this is a personal property of the president. President Corie." Galon's face softened as he spoke.

"He called me *president*," Corie said, her voice shocked. "Not president-elect. Ask him why. Galon is always very proper."

"I am interested, why do you think of her as president?" Cassidy arranged her face in a perplexed expression.

"Because she is. Certainly, you know she's been given the title in absentia? You do not know recent news?"

Galon motioned as though asking permission to come in and Cassidy stepped aside. She glanced at the table where Corie's globe had been set the night before and then realized it pretty much matched the decor of the space anyway. White sculptures were in various places around the cottage, the art supposedly dark and morbid to a culture that valued light and colour so much.

"What?" Corie screamed in her ear.

"What?" Cassidy yelled back.

"Are you okay?" Galon inquired, his face returning to its scowl.

"Sorry, I was just shocked that's all." Cassidy darted

her eyes away at the fib.

"Careful," Corie whispered.

"It's your fault," Cassidy whispered back.

"What's my fault?" Galon asked, wide-eyed now.

"That I'm so easily shocked and that, er, that I'm awake so early."

"You need to be careful," Corie advised.

"I am!" Cassidy said.

"You're what?" Galon's expression now indicated that he thought her a few colours short of a full palette.

"I am unaware of the recent events. My apologies. I've been — er — traveling. That's why I'm here, you know, on my — er — travels. So, I'm...I'm rather tired. And I've had this annoying buzz in my ear..."

"Hey!" Corie exclaimed.

"I understand." Galon gave a half smile, and he wasn't nearly so wild looking when he did.

"Please, catch me up on any news." Cassidy pulled her robe closer and indicated a chair to Galon who pulled it out and settled down into it.

"Thank you. So you see, when President Corie disappeared, there were many who thought the second place winner should be president but Eryn said no. He said that until she is found, she shall remain president as declared by the senate, in absentia. So, without the reversal of the vote of the senate, the parliament will run without a president until the next election."

"And they can do that?"

"Yes, nobody knew the president would be gone this long or I'm sure the senate would have voted different. Only a few voted to put her opponent in place."

"Okay, so she is president still."

"Yes. The opponents are naturally perturbed and are pushing for a new election. Eryn's fearful for his life of course. He gained nothing by opposing them but to become their newest target. And to become the president's Regent."

"Regent? So, acting president. Why do you think the president would disappear in the first place?" Cassidy asked, leaning in, hoping for some insight from this simple man who looked after the property. She knew of course, but what did the people think?

"Most think she was disposed of, that the opponents made her disappear to get the job which is why they're not supportive of the in-absentia decision."

"And the rest?"

"Think she took the key for nefarious purposes and ran away. I cannot, however, think what those purposes would be. But it has vanished as well." He looked pained now. Cassidy noted, this wasn't something he wanted to believe at all.

"What if she were to come back?" she asked.

"If she were to return to us now, she'd be fully the president but, of course, that doesn't help with the key."

"Tell me about the key?"

"The key of Impasto? It disappeared with the president and she is accused by her opponents of stealing it. It would be very difficult to prove she didn't take it."

"What would happen to her if she came back without it?"

"I'm afraid she'd be president but without the key, she would stand trial for stealing it. You really have been travelling a long time?"

"Yes, very long. So, what is this evidence that she has the key?"

"Well, there is the letter supposedly wrote saying she stole it."

"I wrote no such letter," Corie said.

"I don't believe she wrote any such letter," Cassidy said.

"Why not?" He rarely found somebody who thought this way.

"Because if you steal something you don't tell everybody. You hide it," Cassidy said.

"That's right!" Corie said.

"That's a very good point. And one I've made myself. But disappearing made her look even more guilty," Galon responded.

"Can't deny that." Cassidy's mind sifted through the new information.

"Would you like to be imprisoned for life? That's what's going to happen to me, and our prisons are not pleasant places." Corie's voice was sad.

"No," Cassidy said.

"What?" Galon eyed her suspiciously.

"No, problem," she replied in Danch, shaking her head. So Corie had been accused of a crime at the moment of her election but she'd told Dr. Gamgee she was thrown into our world because she was in danger from the opposition. Something was rotten in the State of Denmark. Or rather, Ashlen Der Tenth. And she needed to get to the bottom of it before she went any further.

CHAPTER EIGHT

Galon walked down the pathway and Cassidy watched him leave through the big windows, mind whirling at this recent turn of events. She turned on her heel and went back towards the living room.

"What are you thinking, Cassidy Cane?" Corie's voice jarred her from her thoughts.

"I am thinking that you lied to me." Cassidy whirled around and went to the table, picked up the container holding Corie and turned it so she could see its inhabitant, face to face.

"I did not lie. I just did not say it all."

"It is very important that I have all the information I can when embarking on one of these journeys."

"Well, you do have more than usual, no?" Corie spread her hands, palm up as though to convince her.

"I did not know I was traveling with a person who lies!" Cassidy's eyes flashed with annoyance. "I needed that information."

"I left out a bit of detail. Would you have still brought me if I had told you I was accused of theft?"

"Probably. No, most definitely. Because you still

needed to get back here. Now though, not only am I an outsider but I'm aiding a person charged with criminal activity. Even here, surely that's a crime?"

"Well, your being here at all is a crime," Corie responded. "And if I am president, I can pardon you of everything."

"I have a question. What happens to all those who jump through without glasses? What do your guards do with them?"

"Oh, they receive the worst possible punishment," Corie answered.

"Your prison? Or are they—?"

"They're caught immediately due to their entrancement, then immediately tossed back into your rather dull world."

"Our world isn't dull!" Suddenly Cassidy's affection for her own plane of existence welled up. They had problems, sure, it got boring at times, yeah, but it was a pretty spectacular place, earthside.

"If it is not dull, Cassidy Cane, why do you spend so much time jumping out of it?" Corie inquired.

"That, President, Thief of keys, is none of your beeswax." Cassidy walked across the room, exasperated. This place *was* enthralling, its odd bright and colourful scenery, a blazing glory of beauty unlike any that existed on earth, but it was also *too* jam much. At least for her. For someone like Corie it likely did seem like their world was a muted version, but it suited Cassidy just fine. So why did she spend so much time out of it if it did?

She pondered the question as she dressed, then flitted around in the bright kitchen making food. Why was she here anyway? This was the first time she'd brought something back to a world rather than fetching something. It should have been an advantage having a guide, but it was becoming a challenge, especially since President Corie's instructions interfered with her own very well-honed intuition.

She relaxed her shoulders, inhaled a deep breath and thought about it some more. She pondered how she'd felt the moment before the caretaker had been identified, then after, during her entire conversation with him, she had been fraught with tension. A stress that left her wound up. That tight, agitated feeling had woven itself through her nervous system like a subway winds its way through a maze of tunnels. And she had *loved* it. That's why. It wasn't her preference for other worlds that had her leaving her own so much, it was her love of a good adventure and these adventures were the ultimate rush. Jumping into the unknown, using all her talents, knowledge and skills to retrieve, or replace whatever needed to be retrieved or replaced was the ultimate thrill and she needed it like she needed the water that filled her glass as she poked at the food she'd heated. It was oddly familiar, if a brighter yellow. She picked up the bright purple earthenware jar that had been zapped in some sort of oven as Corie had instructed her. What was this anyway? The jumble of letters assembled into sense during her interpretation of the alphabet, and she snorted. Some things never change, she thought as she pulled out a spoonful of the super bright, and delicious pasta.

CHAPTER NINE

The mac and cheese was excellent for preserved food in a foreign dimension, Cassidy thought. And, as ticked as she was at Corie, they needed to get moving to the presidential residence and return this stupid key that Corie insisted she didn't steal, then somehow reinstate her to her rightful place as president, convince this Eryn guy that she was safe there and to not bottle her up like jelly anymore and then get herself home. Cassidy found it heartening that they only threw interlopers from other paradigms out of the world and back into their own realm, rather than a more permanent solution but, of course, in the past they never got past the lazy guards at the portal. They might not be so merciful with someone aiding and abetting a thief, even if the person they aided happened to be president of their country.

"Snow! It's snowing!" Corie's excited voice exclaimed.

Cassidy grabbed the earpiece and yanked it out. "Don't shout, you'll burst my eardrum!"

"I'm sorry," said a distant voice.

Cassidy replaced the Bluetooth. "That's okay, look,

I'm not pleased you lied about the key and I'm going to need the truth from here on in but what is so interesting about snow? I noticed it had snowed when your caretaker showed up. It's a problem." If Cassidy knew anything, it was that any plans made were always made more difficult, if not impossible upon the arrival of the horrid stuff.

"Look at it, Cassidy. It is the most spectacular thing. You are too far away, go to the outside, open the door!"

Shrugging her shoulders and heading outside, Cassidy braced herself for the cold. The morning sun was masked by the white flakes that flew to and fro outside the door of Corie's cottage. It had already started accumulating and Cassidy was about to close the door and complain about the goose bumps rising on her arms when her eyes caught the glint of colour in the swirls of the flurry. She put her hand out and allowed a few flakes to land on her open palm, then pulled her hand back before they could melt on her warm skin. Each snowflake had the geometrical uniqueness of any snowflake she'd ever observed but instead of being white and silvery the tiny flakes sparkled with colour that glinted and shone in the bright morning light. Then she looked more closely at the blizzard that blew about them and saw within the veils of the cold precipitation, swirling ribbons of rainbows, arching and twisting in the air.

"Oh, my—" Cassidy forgot the cold and stepped outside, nearly as mesmerized by the snowstorm as she'd been by the scene inside Corie's habitat before she'd started wearing the sunglasses.

"It's lovely, is it not?" Corie's voice in her ear asked. They'd not added snow inside her own habitat, there being no time to figure out how to create seasons. "Bring me out!"

"What? Oh, yes. No. After. We can't stand here staring at the snow forever. We need to get moving, get you where you need to be."

"Okay, but you'll need the fast-tracker for the snowy roads, Cassidy Cane. It has snowed all night and piled up."

"The fast-tracker?"

"That's a machine like a scooter but for on the snow."

"So like a snowmobile?"

"Yes, perhaps like that. And you'll need winter wear. The hall cupboard has all of my winter clothes. Take what you need. It will get colder as we go up the mountain, but the snow is timely. We can traverse the winter trail instead of the roads. It'll be a few hours longer but so much more pleasurable and that is the most important thing."

"Is it, Corie? Is it really?" Cassidy rolled her eyes.

"It most certainly is."

"You'll explain some more about the key of Impasto on the way, I trust?" Cassidy asked as she closed the front door, reluctantly blocking the brilliant glitter of shiny flakes outside. She swerved towards the closet and found herself with several one-piece snowsuits in yellow, red and blue. "So much for being camouflaged." She rolled her eyes again and grabbed the red one. This place and it's bright colours. Now she would be whipping up the wintery roads shining like a beacon to all and sundry who saw her along the way. Might as well paint a bullseye on her back and shine a spotlight on it. Why not white? With some pretty sequins to match the outside but oh, no, we must be as bold as a zit on a teenager's nose.

"Are you okay, Cassidy?" Corie asked. "You've been quiet for a long time."

"I'm just thinking how lovely and bright this snow-suit is, Corie." Her voice dripped sarcasm as she finished putting it on and turned to get her backpack for the trip ahead.

***

The snow machine, or Fast-tracker as Corie called the vehicle, looked like a snowmobile with a few variations. It was, of course, a bright scarlet. Its front was pointed, like a snowplow blade. The visor was clear and large and from what Corie told her, did not allow the falling snow to stick to it. The gears were similar to the scooter and after a few runs around the significantly large garden, now blanketed with multicoloured snowbanks, Cassidy had figured them out. Despite her concern over having to travel trails, instead of roads, on an unfamiliar machine, and the pending intrusion of past presidential protectives services, she couldn't help but feel awed by the marvelous precipitation. This place, with its over the top beauty, and weird political priorities, was as fascinating as any place she had ever visited.

And while the miracle that they'd figured out how to create small places that were bigger on the inside, or smaller on the outside if you were the type to borrow prose from popular television programs, was incredible, even that seemed insignificant in moments when the sky burned with red, amber and green and the snow fell in flakes of multicoloured glory.

"Are you ready to go, Cassidy Cane?" Corie asked. Cassidy had wedged her tiny miraculous habitat between windshield and handlebars and lashed it firm with a rope Corie had directed her to in an out-building.

"I am ready to go. So, I am to head straight down the trail and you'll guide me from there on?"

"I will be your guide to the residence, and I will tell you the story as we go."

Like the scooter, the snow machine was quiet. After navigating for ten minutes or so Cassidy felt like she had the driving down pat.

"I'm ready," she told Corie as she sped up a little, eyes fastened on the trail ahead, heart fastened on the beauty of the snow that fell in colourful patterns as she accelerated through the bright purple and blue trees.

"In your world you have computers and things called servers to keep all the information on, true?"

"Yes, that's correct. Pretty much all is digital now. Though we still do have paper files. Wait. Is that what the key of Impasto is?"

"It is a repository and contains all the government files for all of the people. It's the government itself. The president is presented with it upon the showing and induction ceremony. It disappeared before I was due to be presented as president. I was accused of stealing it."

"Why would you steal something you were going to have access to in a few days?"

"They did not notice the theft. A fake was put in its place. That was my defence. But then it was proposed that I had won by taking the key before my election therefore that's why I won, I had an advantage."

"So, there is information in the key that could help you win?"

"Possibly. You see, it holds all the favourite dreams and wishes of all the people, their favourite colours and places, the stories they wish to hear. So having it before the election might well be a big advantage."

"But wouldn't they have noticed it missing before the election?"

"It was replaced so nobody knows exactly of the theft's time. It may have been taken at any time. It was when they went to ready it for presentation that the curator of the files discovered that it was a fake."

"How big is this key of Impasto?"

"It is as small as my hand," she replied.

"You people are good at making small things hold bigger things."

"We call it reductivity. You find that very interesting don't you, Cassidy? I'm glad you do. I too think it is. We have been working on it a long time. Our great President Avvignon Ghenct was really the imaginer of it though. And directed the scientists to create it."

"So, reductivity, not smallerization?"

"It is both. Reductivity is the process whereby smallerization is achieved. It is easy with information. Harder with people and places but we've succeeded."

"Will I be able to learn how it works before I leave?" Cassidy asked.

"I don't even know how it works, that is for the scientists to handle. But I can introduce you to one of them if we're successful."

"You're not interested?" Cassidy asked.

"Once president, I won't have time to be interested in

simple science. I'll be too busy imagining the things I need them to create."

"You know what? You have a strange culture, Corie." She accelerated and the snow machine picked up speed. The reduction helmet kept her ears warm and the wind whipping around her face was brisk. Now that she was getting the hang of it, she realized that this entire part of the journey could be quite fun.

"Faster," Corie encouraged, catching onto her enthusiasm.

Cassidy required no such encouragement. She increased her speed even further, the ungroomed trail smooth beneath the tracks. The wind in her face, the multi-coloured snowbanks on either side of her had her shouting with glee as she took a large turn around a clump of forest.

"Whoohooo!" she bellowed.

Corie laughed in her ear. "I thought you didn't like the winter," she said, wishing she were seated and not encased in a small container like some display statue.

"I like this part," Cassidy yelled, zooming past an outcrop of rock and straightening onto a long, open field where the colourful snowflakes were picked up by the pastel winds and made to dance around before her.

"Corie, who the honeysuckle is that?" she asked at the realization that she'd spoken of her enjoyment far too soon.

"Oh, no, this is not good," Corie said.

"I suspected it wasn't," Cassidy replied wondering what to do next. For there, in the distance stood a shadow that appeared to be a tall man with a weapon slung across his shoulder. And he was waiting for them.

CHAPTER TEN

Surrender!" Corie screamed. "I'm shutting down. Pretend I am but art.

"Surrender? What? Wait, no! Who is it?"

"Pretend you can say you learned about sunglasses from a returning explorer. Whatever you do, they must not see me."

"Perhaps I can escape," Cassidy's words trailed off as another stepped into sight, then another ten, followed by at least another hundred.

"Corie, are you there? Corie?" Cassidy asked, voice desperate as she geared down the machine as the growing army filled her view.

"Great. Just great. Now you shut up." She slowed down the machine, coming to a stop right in front of a woman who appeared to be some sort of military person given that she was surrounded by people wearing identical outfits, bearing arms. The bright blue suits with their sparkling gold buttons were quite attractive, if you managed to ignore that the people wearing it were about to arrest her.

"I am a captain with the president's guard, and you

are an interloper on presidential property. We had a call from Galon, caretaker of Lamartine Cottage," the woman stated. "Come with us."

"But, the machine," Cassidy said, indicating the snowmobile. "And my, er, art." Is that really what you call something that looks abstract, and pretty and completely inanimate and useless, she thought. Well, yes. Good art always had a message and, for certain, Corie could certainly talk your literal ear off, so yeah, art is what it was. Now the question was how to convince the guard to let her take it. Cassidy had forgotten where she was for a moment but was instantly reminded when the guard spoke.

"Art? Of course, you cannot leave your *art* unprotected. Please. Leave the machine, someone will take care of it for you, and you'll come with us."

Cassidy pulled out the receptacle and slipped it into her backpack. The side-eye glance from the guard suggested that she wasn't impressed with Cassidy's particular artistic taste. And that was fine. The less interesting it was the better for both of them.

Cassidy pushed her sunglasses up. Her helmet hid the Bluetooth in her ear for now, though it would appear Corie was implementing radio silence just when she needed her the most. "Thank you. Where are we going, precisely?"

"We are going to the presidential headquarters." the woman said. "I'm Captain Emile Branad. We'll escort you there to investigate your invasion into our territory and decide what to do with you until then."

Cassidy nodded. This was good. She'd be inside the palace which was their ultimate destination though it would be better to have infiltrated on their own terms, not to be a prisoner. And Corie was useless now, her mini-TARDIS had gone black and now it looked like a paperweight with some fancy embossing instead of an entire mini-world. She picked up the *art*. It truly fascinated her that a world so art-based in its philosophies could be so good at science. This thing weighed no more than a five-pin bowling ball but carried a person the size of herself in it. And that person's whole environment. Perhaps she'd get a chance to meet the geniuses who had created the world imagined by a previous president that allowed for the development of this technology. Sure, Corie was president now, but she wasn't the brilliant mind that created big worlds in small places, she just decorated them well with pretty colours and lovely music. And enticing stories.

There were shadows on the cliffs and hills, as Cassidy followed the militia of presidential guards. They caught a gentle breeze and Cassidy, despite the amber vision glasses, found the colours on the snow mesmerizing particularly now that she wasn't driving. The winter chills were diminishing as they descended the mountains. Soon enough they reached a parking lot where she was escorted to another vehicle, this time a boxy car of cornflower blue with a red line across the side. The air was much warmer there and after a few hours of driving the snow disappeared altogether. They drove through the farmland on a brown road that wound its way through fields of grass of blended greens. The grasses were interspersed with rows of flaming flowers that blazed across the landscape and disappeared into the china blue brightness of the hazy sky. Clouds swirled overhead, a blend of violet and lavender, like puffs of pale purple smoke. Champagne and amber grains rose up, waving in the wind, tiny brushes at their tips that seemed to paint the air that changed hue in the swirling breezes.

Cypress-like trees, reaching upwards of a hundred feet in height and created wind-rows along the roadway and leaning against them were tufts of purple irises. The only people she spotted were a group of women in a potato field, and here and there people were binding wheat or picking what appeared to be olives if Cassidy's observations were correct. She couldn't be sure, given her experience with agriculture here was limited and this was an entirely different place.

"Are we there yet?" a voice whispered into her ear and it took a moment for Cassidy to realize that Corie was back online. She glanced at the receptacle in her hand.

"No," She darted a look at the driver. He seemed to not hear her.

"Get to Eryn, he will help. Meanwhile, get news from the guards, talk politics."

"Can you hear me?"

"Yes, I can hear, but I am going quiet again because they must not hear me." Corie's voice trailed off and the globe vibrated in her hand as it shut down once more.

Cassidy checked out the guard who was not totally unfriendly. "So, tell me. I've been out of the loop for a while, what has been going on politically?"

The driver's eyes met Cassidy's in the mirror. "What do you mean? Politically?"

"Well since our president, er, went away, how has it gone? The running of the country?" She had some of this information already, but more was always good, Corie was right on that.

"Oh, that. Terrible. It's a grey time for us. We are ragged men in ragged clothes in the fields. We need to be able to have a new president, but Eryn will not allow it. He says that things must stay as they are until President Corie is declared dead but you can't declare her dead because we don't know if she is."

"Ragged men in ragged fields?"

"What? You do not get a metaphor?"

"I don't get *that* metaphor?" Cassidy said, mulling the words over.

"Are you a scientist?"

Confused, Cassidy considered her answer. The militia leader had called her an interloper. So, she'd assumed she'd been found out as being from another realm. But perhaps not. Perhaps just another country in this realm? Was she still undercover?

"No, just an explorer who has been away." Perhaps bluffing would work. It was worth a shot.

"The ragged men in ragged fields, those without purpose, without light, without art. Once we were ragged, our fields were ragged, nothing was aesthetically pleasing or visually stimulating back then. Until the Anacin seers dreamed of *colourization*. After that things became beautiful, and we advanced greatly. How could an explorer not know these things?"

"Oh, I knew, I just forgot them. So busy, you know, *exploring*."

"Where did you explore?" the driver asked.

"The, er, south," Cassidy responded with the first thing that came to her.

"Oh, lovely there. All those periwinkle beaches."

"Yes, those. Lovely." They *did* sound spectacular. Wow.

"So how does this work? The president is absent, this Eryn is now ruling?" She played dumb.

"With the senators and governors, yes. He's in charge, at least until they figure this out. But people are growing impatient. He hasn't the imagination of the president, he was, after all, just her campaign associate."

"So can't they replace her?"

"He insists she isn't dead. And if she isn't, we can't do anything. It's in the constitution. So it befalls him to govern. But such limited scope and vision. You won't believe this. He wanted to talk about budgets one day. There was much laughter at that. Can you imagine? It was even trending on Squeaker. So embarrassing for us! Anybody can tally numbers. What is required are ideas and creativity. But of course, you know this much. May I ask, why the eyewear?"

"Oh, I have a, er, condition. My eyes are not very pretty to look at, at the moment, so I thought nobody should have to look at them."

"How thoughtful! It's temporary, I hope. Eyes are always the most beautiful part of one's self, don't you agree?"

"Yes, that's why I covered them. *So* embarrassing." Some of this was far too easy now that she was starting to understand. These people loved art and beauty and if she focussed on that she should be able to slide through. She hadn't been picked up for being other-worldly but rather being at the president's cottage. Surely, she could manage to get to Eryn once inside the presidential residence.

CHAPTER ELEVEN

The remainder of the ride was uneventful and enjoyable as far as rides while under arrest went. Cassidy marvelled at the exceptional beauty of Corie's world, particularly this new rural region with fields the colours of gold, yellow, and red as though autumn had grown up from the ground. Further along their drive, more people were out and about. Brightly dressed workers sang shanties in the vast meadows as they laboured, broad smiles on attractive faces, children running through the multicoloured sheaves lain against brightly painted farm tractors. They crossed over a long white bridge that spanned a river of such an exquisite cerulean that Cassidy audibly gasped at its glorious blue then glanced at the driver to see if she had noticed. After all, as a 'local' and an 'explorer' perhaps she shouldn't be as surprised by the beauty of the place as she was.

Soon they entered a city with the most spectacular highways that Cassidy had ever traversed thinking that if she'd driven them herself, she'd have gone off the road, so distracted as she was by their unusual colour. For they were not the dismal grey of asphalt like back home but rather an unusually pale yellow with ribbons of pink and white twisted throughout so that it too was visually exquisite. The painted lines on the roads were a deep red and the rails, where required, were also scarlet and completely visible such that what was entirely a safety feature also beautified the city.

The buildings were also very colourful, but it seemed they were limited to all the hues of blue and green in the world with few variations of bright yellow for contrast. *I'm in a cartoon*, she thought. Except it wasn't cartoonish at all. It was incredibly interesting and beautiful and, yes, artistic.

And entirely dull compared to what came into view a short while later.

For out of the misty clouds that had settled over them in the last fifteen minutes of the drive arose the spires of a castle of silver and crystal that danced and sparkled in the daylight despite the lack of full sunshine. She could see now why they called the presidential residence the Crystal Castle.

"Wow," Cassidy whispered, mouth open in disbelief. And then the sun broke through and suffused the castle in a golden light that sent shards of spectacular colour out from the magnificent building in all directions. The car drove on and Cassidy continued to stare, wide-eyed and mystified at the sheer opulence and glory of the architecture. "They bedazzled the castle," she said aloud. It was as though Disney's castle was amplified by light a million times over into a spectacular display too beautiful for mere humans to even comprehend. She expected fireworks at any moment to explode behind it.

"Have you been here before? On a tour or anything?" The driver asked, knocking Cassidy back to reality.

They approached a tunnel and their vehicle slowed and as it neared the entrance the boxy little car was locked into some sort of rail. The driver cut its engines.

"No, I haven't. I mostly explore the countryside."

"We'll be transported by rail into the presidential residence. It's a security feature, of course. Prevents people from unauthorized entry. Once inside you cannot leave unless you're cleared by the guards to let your vehicle back onto the tracks and only official vehicles can pass through. Everyone is escorted in and out, for safety reasons."

Cassidy was thankful for the tunnel. While it was a lovely shade of mint green it seemed quite boring relative to the exterior of the castle and that was a good thing. She needed to regain her wits. If they need to escape, the only way out was in an official vehicle, she thought. Good to know.

Suddenly the car came to a stop. "Here we are," the guard said. "Follow me."

Cassidy slid out, noticing an item on the dash of the car. With a glance at the guard who was walking away, she reached her hand through the window and nicked it. She wasn't sure what it was, precisely, but if it was what she suspected it might be, it could prove to be very useful at some point in her journey out of this place.

CHAPTER TWELVE

Cassidy had followed along, 'artwork' tucked into her jacket down long corridors that became less and less colourful as they walked, the lovely vine and floral decor giving way to a dull grey as they approached a door with a large box on it. The guard placed their hand in the box and a red light scanned it, then turned green and everything clicked.

With trepidation, she continued. There was nowhere else to go, the hallways seemingly completely sealed off and private. The guard stopped beside another door, repeated the hand scanning and it swung inward.

"In here. You will wait."

"Wait! What?" The room was obviously a jail cell.

"It's where you must wait. Until you are processed."

And then the door shut, and Cassidy was alone in a well-lit room with nothing to see. Except a low cot and another door. She opened it and inside were bathroom facilities but nothing more. She closed it again.

She walked over and sat on the cot. How long would she be here? Was it safe to take the glasses off? The guard didn't seem to object to her wearing them.

She pulled Corie out of her coat and set the globe? on the bed. "Corie. We're here in jail. Can you Open Sesame or something?"

A few moments later a slow buzz was audible and a second later Corie appeared in the little window. Cassidy adjusted it so that soon it appeared that Corie sat before her.

"You are inside the presidential residence?" she inquired.

"Yes, I'm here in a jail cell it appears. How do I get them to take me to Eryn though? I have no idea how to make that happen. To them I'm just a lowly prisoner who is in jail for trespassing on your property. Surely, they won't let me speak to him. It'll be all judges and juries and such, right?"

"Yes, that is a good point, Cassidy Cane. But it is Eryn I must see."

"There is no escaping this cell. The only thing I can think of is to confess to a crime that gets me an audience with your old pal Eryn. What is the crime that would do that? Or is there such a thing?"

"I don't know. Perhaps treason? Yes, I think that is the only one."

"Treason, oh boy. That sounds serious."

"It is. If found guilty it will get you locked alone in a dingy room forever."

"So I'm risking being locked up forever on the odd chance it might get me to see Eryn?"

"Yes, I am afraid so."

Cassidy mulled it over. She had to do something, but this was awfully risky. What if there was no way out? They didn't even know she was from outside but what if they discovered this. She supposed she could throw herself on the mercy of the court. It wouldn't be treason if she wasn't from the place she was accused of it in, right?

"I have an idea! You need to pretend to know of a treasonous act, offer to tell them all about it but say you will only tell Eryn?" Corie said.

"That *is* brilliant! Yes, that might work. Well done, Corie!"

"I'm not just a pretty faceted snow globe you know," Corie responded.

Cassidy laughed. "Who knew you had such a sense of humour! That's funny!"

"It is?" Corie asked. "Why?"

Cassidy's laughter tapered off. With a final chuckle, she said, "another time. Now, how do I call somebody?"

"There should be a button to summon the guard."

Cassidy stood and walked to the door. She patted the walls until she found a slight depression in the wall almost like a dent but subtler. Of course, switches weren't aesthetically pleasing so they hid them.

"This?"

"That's it," Corie said. "I shall shut down. You may have to push two or three times to get heard."

Cassidy pushed on it and nothing happened. She waited a while before she pushed again. Then she heard steps outside in the hallway. They stopped and then the door slid open.

"How may I assist you?" Captain Emile Branad asked.

"I need to see Eryn." Cassidy demanded.

"You can't see Eryn. You will be processed soon and sent to community court."

"I need to report a treason against him, and I need to do it now. It is of vital importance and I will not tell anyone *but* Eryn."

"Treason?" The guard's eyes opened wide.

"Yes, of the worst kind. A coup. Yes, that's it. Somebody is trying to take over the country and I need to tell him before it is too late. I was sent on a diplomatic mission from...er...another country to tell him."

"Say it's Saged." a voice said into her ear.

"Saged. The country of Saged. Gades, its mayor is the problem."

"City!"

"City of Saged, I mean."

The guard's eyes narrowed.

"Why were you at the cottage of President Corie, then?"

"Tell them because Galon invited you there." whispered Corie.

"I was invited there by Galon. He is good friends with president-elect Corie, and I must see Eryn now. To tell of the coup. It's an emergency." Cassidy stood tall, trying to look imposing and important, whatever that might look like in this country.

"I'm no fool. Galon was the one who called us and told us you were there. And if this treason was the case, why not say so at the cottage?" asked Captain Branad.

"Yes, because, er, I told Galon to call you. Because I needed to be sure I could get into the residence first. I also had to know that you could be trusted. You seem like an upstanding and loyal guard. And remember, I did not realize you would lock me in jail."

"Where did you think we would put you for trespassing? In the kitchen?"

"So, everybody's a comedian now?"

"Well, it was a silly thing to say." A twinkle flecked in the guard's eye.

"Okay, it was." I think I'm getting through to her, Cassidy thought. "Will you please take me to see Eryn. Imagine what will happen if you don't and this terrible coup occurs. It will be on your shoulders. I can't even—"

Cassidy turned away from Captain Emile Branad and sat on the bed. She waved a hand as though to dismiss the guard who was pondering the choice before her.

The guard thought carefully. If she took this prisoner to Eryn and it was nothing she'd be reprimanded and perhaps lose rank or even her job. However, if she didn't take her and it proved to be such a terrible thing, well, she might end up in the grey dungeon for her entire life. A coup would destroy the country, ruin everything and things were already bad since the uproar after the president's disappearance.

"Okay, bring your things and follow me to Eryn's quarters. He *is* in at the moment but may be busy. Be patient and wait. And please keep on those glasses. He does not need to see imperfect eyes today."

"Yes, certainly." Cassidy grabbed Corie's receptacle and placed it inside her coat. She followed the guard who walked briskly down the corridors. It took a long time to get to the elevator and then another ten minutes to get to the end of the elevator's journey at the very highest floor of the residence.

Once there, Captain Branad entered a series of numbers, placed her face in a scanner and responded, "transporting a witness for review by Regent Eryn."

"We were not expecting anybody," a voice said.

"Picked up today. Says she has word of a planned treason. A coup. By Gades, mayor of Saged."

"What? A coup? That's very serious. Of course, yes. Absolutely, please, bring her in."

"Keep me hidden," Corie whispered in her ear. "I want to listen to what Eryn says before I am freed. Also, look for a pedestal. It is very important to find a stand upon which I can belong."

"Okay, got it."

"Pardon?" Emile Branad asked.

"Just practicing in my mind how to tell Eryn about the problem," Cassidy said looking around at the beautifully decorated walls. The interior of the building was extraordinary yet somehow subdued relative to the natural environment outside its walls but wasn't that normal for all places? Gathering intel on the structure and searching for ways out, should escape be required, she noted there was an exit and large windows. The windows were useless as they were so high up, but perhaps the door would be a way to leave if she had to run.

"I will let the APO know you're here."

"APO?"

"Acting president's office."

"Oh, yes. Thank you." She noted the difference in labels. Not regent but acting president. Was Eryn a beneficiary of Corie's disappearance. It was worth considering that he might actually be the bad guy here.

"Sit over there."

Cassidy was directed to a chair and then the captain went to a corner and picked up some sort of communication device. She couldn't make out the words.

"They're arguing. I'm not sure if we'll get in," Cassidy said, knowing Corie could hear.

"You're in," the captain said. "Let's go."

"Oh, well, never mind then. I mean, sorry, yes of course. Let's go."

This time the door was opened from the inside and she was told to enter without Captain Branad.

"The president's secret service will take it from here," a guard in bright yellow uniform said. "Come through. The acting president wishes to see you now. You have five minutes to state your case."

"Thank you." Cassidy's heart thumped. This was it. Now, what the heck was she supposed to say. She'd just have to wing it.

Cassidy was led to a large door and the new guard, a stern looking older man, walked to the screen. His face was scanned, and the door slid across. He took Cassidy by the elbow and guided her through.

A siren sounded and Cassidy put her hands over her ears although they were somewhat protected from the earpieces she wore.

"What is that?" she yelled.

"The security alarms. What do you have with you that set them off?" The guard yelled at her.

The alarms stopped suddenly.

"I know what she has," a man's voice said in the sudden quiet.

"You do?" Cassidy asked, taking her hands off her

ears.

"Yes, I do. Would you come with me?"

Cassidy followed him inside. There was a half-dozen people in the room, it appeared that a meeting had been in session. "Give me the room," Eryn said as though they were in an episode of a TV show and it worked. They all stood and left with a curious glance at Cassidy and a handshake to their acting president.

Once they were gone, Eryn looked at Cassidy.

"So, where is she?" he asked.

"Who?" Cassidy responded, confused look on her face.

"Don't play with me. You know who."

"He knows. You will have to let me out. But you must put me on the stand beside his desk. I can only extrapolate from there."

"Well?" Eryn asked folding his arms across his chest.

"I am Cassidy Cane and I came to tell you about a coup against you by Gades, mayor of the city of Saged. Sure, I don't even know what you're talking about. But wow! What a nice place." Cassidy wandered, feeling Eryn's eyes on her back. She looked at a painting of a tall woman. "Is she your wife?" she asked knowing darned well it was Corie in the painting.

"She is our former president. She is no longer with us." Eryn's sad look could easily be a ruse. These people were artists and acting was an art form. She reached into her jacket and placed her hand on the container with Corie in it. Out of the corner of her eye she saw Eryn lunge and knew the jig was up. Reflexes sharp as a cat she leapt forward, and Eryn went sprawling past her. Spinning on her heel, she turned and headed towards the large, red desk.

"On the stand. I must go on the stand!" Corie said. "It's imperative."

"Shut up, I've got this," Cassidy said, making a dash across the large room towards what looked like a tall candle holder with four corner pieces in which the canister that held Corie would fit perfectly. No time to think, a movement out of her eye had her barrelling towards it.

"What are you doing?" Eryn sped towards her but, globe clenched in her fist Cassidy reached out toward the stand with it just as Eryn grasped her by the tail of her jacket.

"No!" She wrenched forward and escaped his clenched hand. In the moment before he grabbed her again, she placed the faceted globe that held President Corie inside it, on the ornate stand as requested.

"There, you're back!" Cassidy screeched as she was hauled back by Eryn and pushed aside while he ran forward screaming, "No!"

But a great cloud of white smoke and an explosion that vibrated through the room sent him flying backwards.

He grabbed Cassidy and twisted her arm behind her back. There was a loud whistling noise. Cassidy struggled to free herself while Eryn held on tight. Cassidy's struggle stopped and Eryn's grasp loosened as the fog cleared.

The voice in Cassidy's ear now filled the room. Corie stepped forward and stood before them, once more in her own real world and ready to take her role as president of the country of Impasto.

"I am back," Corie's voice was strong and she shocked Cassidy when she said, "And you, Eryn, are under arrest for high treason against the president and country of Impasto."

CHAPTER THIRTEEN

Eryn twisted Cassidy's arm and she pulled hard to try to escape.

"Treason. Guards, guards!" Corie shouted.

Several presidential guards rushed into the room. They brought up short at the sight of President Corie and Eryn holding Cassidy in a vice-like grip as she struggled to free herself. They took a step, in unison, as though to go towards Eryn.

"I am not a criminal," Eryn claimed. "Let me go, we can sort this out."

Corie raised a hand. "I am the duly elected president and I have the right to take my place as such. Eryn only stood in my absence and law must decide who is rightful, not guards. Stand down now. Cassidy has brought me back, you must protect her, grab Eryn who cast me from this land, and remove him to the grey room."

The guards looked at Corie, then at each other, nodded at each other and moved towards Eryn.

"No! Please. Corie, I did what I had to do. Then we shall work it out. Please, guards, for now, I am president."

The guards stopped to consider his word. They looked at each other again, seemed to come to some agreement and moved towards Corie as if to grab her.

"No! Stop! He is a liar. He threw me into the canister of smallness, to hide me, perhaps until he could get the key. He claimed there was an impending coup and that I was in danger. Yes, he fooled me, and now he's trying to fool you." She insisted. "I thought he was a friend, so I did as he suggested. Now I realize he probably just wanted the power himself. Again, *I* am the president. People voted for me, *not* Eryn. And I am the one who must oversee the search for the key of Impasto. It is not in my possession, but I am the president. Take him away. Now!"

The guards again looked at each other, sizing up the situation. A few moments seemed eternal until they finally nodded and seemed firmer in their decisiveness. They marched towards Eryn who still held Cassidy by the arm.

"What of the other prisoner, President Corie?" The tallest of the two guards asked.

"Release her to me. She aided my return and is a very important person to help locate the key."

"Stay away from me," Eryn ordered helplessly, pulling Cassidy closer. "Corie, you have it wrong, I—"

"Oh, enough," Cassidy said. She stomped her foot down hard on his. He let out a howl of pain and loosened his grip on her. Cassidy maneuvered herself free, turned and grabbed his thumb, and twisted it until he released her arm fully. She kept winding it until he went to his knees begging her not to break it off from his hand altogether.

The impressed guards moved in and lifted him off the floor as Cassidy stood by, rubbing the ache in her shoulder from where it had been wrenched. She watched as Eryn was led out and the door shut behind them.

Finally, alone in the room, Cassidy turned to Corie.

"Are you okay? I wasn't sure you understood that Eryn was likely not honest with you," she said as she noted the greyish tinge to her skin and an expression of angst on her face.

"Yes, it's unfortunate he turned out to be a crook. But mostly I feel bad from the extrapolation. Largerization is not pleasant. I must lay down. I will summon my senators soon but before I do, please search the cupboards for absinthe. I need a restorative drink.

Cassidy opened a few cabinet doors, and it took only a short while to find a bottle and glasses. She filled a goblet and returned it to Corie who lay on a long settee propped against a large window overlooking the city.

"Thank you, Cassidy Cane, for this and the return. Will you not join me?" She sipped on the absinthe and closed her eyes in ecstasy at its taste.

She wrinkled her nose. "I think I'll pass. So, that's it? You're home and you're president, just like that? I can leave?"

"Not quite, Cassidy Cane. Your work here is not done. We now need to find the key. I don't have it, so where is it?"

"Oh right. This makes things difficult. Because whoever took the key doesn't appear to be in cahoots with Eryn."

"And also, they're not working with him."

"But that's the same — nevermind," she pulled the earpiece out of her ear. She didn't need it anymore now that Corie was right sized. She pushed the glasses up, however. Just in case, because this room was awfully bright and pretty.

"We must return it to me. From whoever has it."

"The question is, who has it? Any ideas?"

"Yes, unfortunately I think I do know who might have it."

"Who?"

Corie sipped the absinthe drink, gave a big sigh, and pondered before answering. "I can only think of one person who would have taken the key."

"Who? For the love of cookie dough, spit it out."

"Gades. The mayor of Saged."

"Explain further please. That's the name you asked me to use to get out of the cell," Cassidy said, moving about the room, looking at books and art. "I'm dying to know who he is and why he might have the key."

CHAPTER FOURTEEN

"Gades, the mayor of Saged, was my primary opponent in the presidential election. A man of very small imagination and you know, in presidential elections, the size of a man's *imagination* is very important."

"I *imagine* it is," Cassidy said, stone-faced.

"He lost. The defeat was large. But he didn't lose well. He was angry although he acted as though he was conciliatory, I could tell."

"And you suspect he's tangled up in this? Do you really think they're possibly in on it together and maybe Gades double-crossed Eryn?"

"I can't say for sure. Eryn acted as my friend, told me that a coup was coming. That Gades was angry and wanted to contest my win. He was accusing me of cheating, of all sorts of things but would he feel better if Eryn were president? It gives him no power."

"But perhaps the power is in having the key. Wouldn't it be too obvious if he jumped into trying to be president. Perhaps he was in on you being sent out of the realm, into ours, and then the goal was Eryn to act in your stead until they had an election to replace you. But Eryn got greedy and decided to stay, claiming you would come back. But without the key, he couldn't function properly. To tell everyone Mayor Gades had it would be to admit being a traitor?" Cassidy paced the room, thinking.

"Perhaps. Something isn't right though, but I can't think what I'm missing here." Corie said. "But then, I trusted Eryn, so I'm not reliable anyway."

"So what's next? Go after Gades?"

"I think so, yes, but after I meet with the senate. They must be addressed first, to let them know I've returned, and that Eryn is no longer in charge and, in fact, is incarcerated."

"Surely, they know now, right? I mean there were people here who have probably spread the word."

"Yes, but I must formally invite them. I will do that now. An emergency session." She drained the remainder of the absinthe from her glass with a huge sigh of appreciation. Then she stood and walked to the large desk in the middle of the room and picked up a round object.

"Principal Senator Theo, this is President Corie. Please direct the other senators to attend to the chambers immediately for an emergency meeting of the senate to discuss my kidnapping, return, and the arrest of Eryn Shrub." She clicked a button and laid it back down. A knock came on the door.

"That was fast."

"Too fast."

"Stay here," Cassidy instructed striding towards the door. "Who is it?"

"The PSS. We are here to help President-elect Corie."

Cassidy looked towards Corie who nodded her consent. Cassidy opened the door a smidge and peeked out to see the two guards from earlier.

"You are alone?"

"Yes, and we are here to protect President Corie. We recognize her as the true and proper inhabitant of this office. Please allow us to continue our jobs as her protectors."

"Come in then," Corie said, her voice strong and presidential.

"Thank you, Ma'am," the taller guard said. "You may not remember me, but I was there when you were elected. It was a happy day."

"It was for me too," the other guard piped up. "I voted for you."

"Shhhh, we are to be impartial," the first admonished.

"That's okay. We'll let propriety go for now. I need loyal guards to protect me, and our democracy, and I appreciate your vote. And your help. I have a senate meeting now. But I am reclaiming my power and my first action is to promote you both as my official guards. I don't know why, but I trust you. You made the right decision when you were called on to do so and that bears rewarding. Now I require you in your new official capacity as bodyguard to the president duties to escort me and my adviser, Cassidy Cane of America, Earthside, to the senate chambers. There we will start to sort out this entire mess. Does that sound fair?"

The two guards puffed up and stood straight. They touched their chins in unison, something Cassidy presumed was a type of salute and nodded.

"I am delighted to accept your promotion and will guard you with my body and soul," the shorter guard said.

"Thank you, what is your name?"

"I am Raph and this is Micho," he replied nodding to the taller guard.

"Pleased to meet you both. Let's go, shall we?"

"Wait, Ma'am, I don't mean to interfere but should you not, you know, apply the sash of incumbency?"

"Oh, yes. You are correct. Thank you."

Cassidy watched, curious as Corie went to a small table near the window where an ornate box sat. She flipped open the lid and pulled out a folded length of fabric, unwound it and slipped it over her head, brushing the front of it with her hand. She closed the lid and turned with a broad smile.

"Feels official now," she said. The sash read **President** and naturally, was adorned with embroidered sunflowers and stars.

"That's very nice. Shall we go through?" Cassidy said, not quite so taken with the pomp of things as the two guards who again did their strange chin salute which Corie returned with grave reverence on her face.

"Yes, yes. Of course. Guards. Lead the way, please."

Raph walked out and Corie followed. Micho indicated that Cassidy should go next, and he brought up the rear as they made their way to the chambers where Corie would take back control of her country and Cassidy would try to figure out who or what had the darned key of Impasto that she was supposed to return to President Corie.

CHAPTER FIFTEEN

The senate chamber room was as ornate as the sash and decorated in a similar style with gold trimmed murals of amber fields of wheat and bright yellow sunflowers bedecking the walls. The windows were broad and high and overlooked the city and Cassidy shoved her glasses up on her nose as she was escorted into the room to prevent her from falling into a trance over it all. The massive room had benches on both sides for the senate to sit at, but Cassidy was led on through to another room with a long boardroom table and collection of chairs that were now mostly filled. The brightly dressed senators, animated and loud, went dead quiet when the four of them entered the room. The guard stepped aside and allowed Corie to lead. She strode across the room and sat in the chair at the head of the large table. Gone was the nervous passenger in a strange canister depending on another to bring her home. There, instead, sat a strong woman ready to take back her rightful place as president of her country. Cassidy chewed the inside of her cheek and pondered the transformation as she stood with the guards on the sidelines. Perhaps smallness inside the pod had created smallness within Corie. She sure seemed larger than life at the head of the table now.

"You, there. Move! My advisor will sit there," Corie instructed a senator who stood, and moved to a vacant chair with a look in her eyes as though she'd been ordered to move by a ghost. Or perhaps a demon. Either way there was no disputing the authority Corie now carried.

Cassidy slipped into the chair feeling all eyes in the room on her. She tucked her hands beneath the table and clasped them tight to help resist the urge to remove her hair from its ponytail to look more formal and govern-mental, given the serious looks she was being sent. She was an archaeologist, not a presidential adviser, which might not be a popular vocation in a room that might contain enemies of that president.

"Call to order," Corie said, her voice strong. Every head turned towards her, anxious to hear what she had to say. They knew she weaved a lovely tale and part of it was curiosity but part of it was the anticipation of a good long story.

"Please just ask me questions. That's what I request," she said, solemn.

"Why did you run away?"

Cassidy jerked her head towards the speaker, a short woman with long brown hair and a serious expression.

"I ran for my life. At least that's why I thought I left. I was convinced that it was best for the country if I left for a while. Perhaps that was the right choice, perhaps not, that remains to be seen but it was at the encouragement of my former adviser, Eryn, who has now been arrested for treasonous acts."

"Why? Where have you been? How did you escape?" the same woman asked.

"Your question is valuable, LaFont." she skipped over it and answered in her own way. "It's difficult to admit that I was duped. I trusted him completely, he had helped me become elected and I believed his lies about a coup and so, when under the guise of protecting me, he suggested I run, I reluctantly agreed. He promised to fix the problem and return me to power. Now it seems that in my absence he blamed me for stealing the key of Impasto and acted as president. But he has not been a good or rightful president. And as the legal president I have taken back my position and Eryn will remain in the grey room until his trial."

Cassidy glanced around as Corie talked. Eryn must not have acted alone, and she scanned the crowd for anyone who didn't seem surprised by this story.

"Where *is* the key then? It's gone and it disappeared when you did!" A man with stark white hair interrupted and his question was echoed by the rest of the gathered assembly.

"Tonem! I do not have the key! I never had it."

"But there was a letter of confession. Eryn showed us in the senate. And if you don't have it, who does? Where is it?" Tonem asked. He seemed to have a leadership role and the others waited for Corie's answer.

"I did not write that letter. It was forged and I repeat, I do not know. And the interesting thing is I don't think Eryn knows either."

"You don't?"

"No, he would have been a better leader with it." She

looked at Cassidy who nodded.

"So, we are to believe you now after you ran away and deserted us?"

"I had bad advice. I will get better advice from here on in." Corie's voice was strong.

"From your new," he gave Cassidy a derisive look, "advisor?"

"Yes. From me," Cassidy said. "And my advice right now is to end this inquisition and instead we go question the prisoner, Eryn."

"I think we get to say who gets to—"

"You get no say at all," Corie told him. "Cassidy Cane is right. We're going to see Eryn and we're going to do it now. Dismissed."

The senators looked open-mouthed from Corie to Cassidy, then to Tonem, then slowly rose to do as they'd been ordered.

"Corie, you're bossy as heck as president," Cassidy said.

"I'm a leader, Cassidy. Bossiness is a requirement. Come on, let's go see Eryn."

CHAPTER SIXTEEN

Eryn sat in the small grey room, face in his hands. The door slid open, and President Corie walked in with Cassidy Cane at her side. He looked up at them, bright blue eyes awash, red-rimmed. He wiped his eyes and stood.

"Cor — President Corie. Why are you here?" He waved his arm around to indicate the cell.

"To question you. Where is the key, Eryn?" Corie demanded, hands on her hips as though she were his mother scolding him for leaving a mess about.

"I do not know. I swear."

"I do not believe you. I have no reason to."

"I really do not, Corie. And if you don't, I must truly and humbly apologize. I truly thought you might have stolen it. The letter was *so* real. It looked to be in your beautiful cursive. I was absolutely certain you tricked me. When I removed you for your own safety, I thought I was doing the right thing. Then the letter came and I was sure you had it."

"What good would it have been to me in another world?"

"That's the part I couldn't figure out." Eryn

shrugged.

"So you saw this as an opportunity for you to take power?" Corie asked.

"Power? Corie, I've never desired power. I have only ever desired — well, I decided to stand as your regent, then acting president, because I was hopeful someday, I could get to you, perhaps get you back. And I did try. I went out into the other realm, I searched all around the area but there was no sign, no clue as to where you had gone."

"I'm guessing Professor Gamgee already had picked you up by then." Cassidy propped her forefinger under her chin, contemplating his explanation.

Eryn looked at Cassidy with renewed interest. "You are from the other realm and you are helping President Corie return to her place as president?"

"Yes, that's the goal. Which is complete but I'll stick around to find that key of yours as well. It seems like Corie won't get to be president for long if it's not found.

"Without it there will always be suspicion. If we don't find it whoever takes the presidency is doomed, I believe," Eryn said.

"Yes, I can see that. Plus all those people's private information in the wrong hands—"

"Wait! You believe him, Cassidy Cane?" Corie looked shocked.

"I — well it sounds plausible. I'd like to hear his entire explanation before I decide."

Eryn nodded and encouraged, continued. "I knew you were resourceful and would come back if you could, President Corie. And I was right." He looked at Corie as though he still couldn't believe his eyes that she was there.

Cassidy noticed something else about Eryn. An expression in his eyes. What was it? Then it dawned on her. This was a man smitten. Eryn was in love with Corie. And she seemed clueless to that fact. And if he was, did that make him more or less of a suspect? If he loved her, he'd hardly betray her, but if she rejected him, revenge for an unrequited love could be a motive.

"But then when I arrive you attacked Cassidy and tried to prevent my extrapolation?" Corie snapped.

"Because of the letter. It came after you were gone. I thought you had betrayed me — the country, I mean. I thought when you returned you would have the key, would have had it all along, and had stolen it like they said. And that you possibly had used it to cheat to win the election."

"If you thought she was a cheater, I mean, cheated to get the election, why didn't you just let the opponent take power?" Cassidy leaned in, looking closer at his face to see his answer in his eyes as well as hear it.

"Because I still — I didn't want to believe it. I thought I was better for the country because I am not under the thumb of Mayor Gades and even if I am not a good president, I am better than he would have been."

"I have heard that the people are not satisfied with your governance," President Corie said.

"Of course they are not. I can't inspire like you. A president needs to be a muse to the people. I'm not that. If I were, I would have run myself. I know my flaws. I just wanted to support the best person to run the country and that was you. My — our afflatus president."

"Afflatus?" Cassidy ran the word through her brain. She had amazing translation abilities. Unfortunately, a dictionary hadn't come with that upload.

"It is another word for a muse. It's the best kind of president to have. One who is both artist *and* muse and Corie was held up as the first candidate to be such a president in a long time. Perhaps that's why they framed her, stole the key, sent the letter and tried to stop her from becoming president."

"Perhaps," Cassidy said. "Here is my confusion, Eryn. If you thought Corie was going to find her way back, and would figure all this out, why did you encourage her to leave in the first place. Why couldn't she have stayed and together you could have figured this out? Surely the guards could and would have protected her."

"I didn't know which guards to trust, and the threatening letters suggested that the only way to protect her was to hide her away."

"But Eryn, your job was not to protect me, it was to serve the country," Corie said.

"I know but you were my priority, and yes the country was also a priority, but I put you first. Perhaps I made a wrong choice, I probably should have listened when you objected. I know it looks like I tried to steal your presidency, but I did not. I just thought I could protect you and figure this out before you arrived back. Instead, I've been so distracted by taking care of the country and saving the presidency that I've failed to make this place any safer for you."

"Oh, it's safer for her," Cassidy said. "I'm here now

and we'll get this sorted before I leave. That is a guarantee."

Eryn and Corie looked at Cassidy and then back at each other. A look passed between them, a flicker like a tiny firefly dancing just out of reach then disappearing. But Cassidy caught it before it vanished.

These two were far more than candidate and campaign manager and she would get the rest of this story from Madame President Corie as soon as she possibly could.

CHAPTER SEVENTEEN

"So, you and Eryn, in love huh?" Alone with Corie again, Cassidy leaned back and looked around the office, nonchalant as she asked the question.

"Cassidy Cane!"

"Oh, come on. I've been trying to figure out why you would listen to him when you could have stayed behind and defended yourself. And I've been trying to figure out why he was so determined to save you by doing that if he wasn't after your power. And that has to be it. You're in love with each other. Admit it. Fess up."

"It is personal."

"You brought me here to find your blasted key. There is no such thing as personal. I need to know everything. Are you in love or involved in some other way?"

"I need a drink." Corie made her way across to the absinthe bottle, poured a generous glassful and sat back down at her desk. Cassidy was lounging in the big arm chair on its opposite side, leg draped over one arm trying to figure out their next move.

"You have your drink. Now tell me."

"I confess I do have certain feelings for Eryn that may

have impacted my judgment."

"Ha! I knew it!" She sat upright. "You two were locking lips and looking for votes. Was it a scandal? Or did you manage to hide it away?"

"We were not, locking the lips! We were completely professional. As his superior it was not right for me to entertain a romantic relationship. It would be completely wrong."

"But you fell in love all the same. And he has feelings for you as well. It is the only thing that makes sense unless he really does want to be president, but he doesn't seem to."

"If he has such feelings, he hasn't said so. So, you think? Do you really think he does?" Corie was casual in the question, but her eyes were eager.

"He's smitten like a kitten."

"What does that mean?"

"That he likes you. He '*like*' likes you." She wiggled her eyebrows. "For real, in a romantic way. But also more, I think he truly cares for you and that even if romance is off the table he really loves you, so he did what he did to protect you, as misguided as that was."

"Do you think he really searched for me in your world?"

"I imagine so. He seemed sincere and it is true, you were gone fairly quickly after."

"That would have been dangerous, we've never been sure we could survive out there. There were stories, though some say they were made up fables to keep us from trying."

"Maybe he cared enough to risk it?"

"Wow. I never thought of that. Should we let him out of jail maybe?"

"No, we have no proof. We need to figure out who has the key and prove him, and you, innocent. Then you guys get married and have little presidential babies."

"Cassidy Cane!" Corie giggled. "You are a tease."

Cassidy grinned. "Perhaps so. Anyway, this is all interesting but still doesn't help us figure this out. Our prime suspect is Mayor Gades of Saged. Would you agree?

"Yes, so how do we get him to confess?"

"Well, by now he will be aware you are here. Maybe we need to pull a bluff," Cassidy thought.

"What is a bluff and how does one pull it?" Corie asked.

"I will explain. Then we will start to implement the plan. Do you have something similar to a press conference here?"

"Where we call the media and they come and hear announcements? We have those."

"Can you call one?"

"Yes, of course. I'm sure all the media is eager to hear about where I've been and why I'm back."

"Okay, then here is what we're going to do. And we may need one of your artists to help out."

And Cassidy set about explaining her plan to a very skeptical president.

CHAPTER EIGHTEEN

The crowd had gathered before the dias. Microphones surrounded the podium. It was very much like a press conference back in the earth realm except for the microphones being painted in bright colours with intricate patterns and the podium glittering with crystals that sparkled in the sunlight. Cassidy pushed her shades up to ensure she was not distracted by all the colours and glittery sights. The media room was all windows and the view over the city was breathtaking and likely spellbinding to a non-bespectacled Cassidy.

"Okay, I am ready. Eryn will surely hate me for this when I am finished."

"He will not. But even if he were to, country first. This will help you and Eryn. Now get out there."

Corie entered the room. The chattering voices stilled at her entrance and all was quiet as she made her way, flanked by her two loyal guards to the podium. Cassidy followed behind, standing just to the left of the stage in order to keep a wide look at the gathered reporters.

"Good evening fellow citizens," Corie began. Cameras snapped as she began her address.

"I have returned to take over my position as president of the country. My decision to be away for so long was improperly advised and I apologize for my absence. I could give a big, long speech but I sense you have questions for me, and I think that we are best to proceed with those without hesitation. Just know that I am here to answer as best I can. Please go ahead."

"Where were you?" The first question came from a lady with white hair in the first row.

"I was in a safe place until things settled down. It was so safe that I do not want to reveal it in case others need to be protected in the future."

"Did you steal the key of Impasto?" a young fellow with a bright yellow jacket asked.

"I did not," Corie responded.

"Was there really a letter from you confessing that you stole it?"

"There was a letter saying that, but it was a forgery. I did not write that letter."

"Nonsense, you wrote the letter, and you stole the key and used it to win the election."

"Does that make sense? I stole the key to win the election, then after winning I disappear with it instead of becoming president, then I write a letter confessing that I did that. To what end? What would I have to gain?"

The reporters became silent. They were logical thinkers, and she was right, it didn't make sense.

"So why have you called us here today? There was to be some sort of announcement?"

"Yes, I came today to announce that the key of Impasto has now been located and will be returned to us very shortly."

Cassidy watched the room. Several senators who were present sat near the back shuffled about. One of them slipped out. She nodded at the guard who left the stage while the reporters shouted words at her.

"Where is it?" One asked.

"Why was it stolen?" Another shouted.

"Has anybody been arrested?"

Corie handled them all like a pro, tossing out answers as best she could while giving absolutely nothing away. "Definitely a politician," Cassidy thought as she slipped from the stage.

She rushed around to the foyer where the guard was engaged in a discussion with the man who had slipped out. He looked vaguely familiar, and she remembered him from the meeting with the senators.

"I will be reporting this to the president, she'll have your job for treating me this way," he said.

"What do we have here, Raph?" Cassidy inquired.

"You! Who are you, anyway, that you are suddenly advising the president? Do you know we can't find out who she is? We do not know where this traveller comes from? Her name does not exist in—"

"In the key?"

The man's eyes darted back to Raph, then Cassidy.

"How could you even search my name if it's missing?" Cassidy asked.

"Yes, Senator Zwart. How could you?" Raph asked.

The senator looked from Raph to Cassidy and back again. Then he darted away.

"Oh, no you don't," Cassidy said as she took a dash

towards the door after him. Raph made chase as well but the senator was faster and was through the door as Cassidy came up to it. She rushed through and picked up speed with Raph just a few feet ahead of her. Then suddenly her legs were shot out from underneath her and she tumbled like a bowling ball, rolling to bring herself upright to her feet but instead of continuing the chase she stood stock still, mesmerized by the crystal glow of the walls of the presidential palace, the cornflower blue of the sky and the opulent marvels of a nature that was so incredibly beautiful it left her in its enthrall, sunglasses having been knocked clear off her face in her fall.

Raph continued his chase but Cassidy was unaware as she leaned forward to smell a fragrant blossom, her thoughts only on the scene around her.

"Cassidy!" Micho shouted from behind her. She did not acknowledge him.

"What is wrong with her, Madam President?" He asked, circling around an entranced Cassidy who stood marvelling at the flowers.

"She dropped her glasses. Grab them. Put them on her face."

"Corie, look at the pretty flowers. They smell so nice."

"Put them on her, Micho, fast!" Corie ordered.

"You're very handsome," Cassidy said to the guard, placing a hand on his cheek. "Isn't he particularly adorable?" she asked to the dismay of the mortified guard.

"Quick, put the glasses on her now!"

"Yes, Madam President." The confused guard placed them on Cassidy's face as she looked at him adoringly.

"You're just one of the best looking guards I ever saw—" Cassidy pushed up the glasses and suddenly she could focus again.

"Oh, my God," her hand dropped. "I let him get away!" She turned, already recovered, unlike the guard, Micho, who she'd been complimenting moments earlier.

She took off towards where Raph had disappeared only to see him coming with the senator, hands locked together with what appeared to be a bright yellow strap.

"In the back door. Before the reporters realize what's been going on. You played the video?"

"Yes, we wanted to give adequate time with them distracted but we only have a few minutes, let's take him up to my office."

Cassidy followed behind them, the guard looked at her sheepishly, but she pretended nothing had happened, offering a cool smile as she walked past him. She was as mortified as he was when she realized what had happened, but she certainly wasn't going to address that here and now. No sirree, best pretend the entire episode hadn't occurred. I mean, he was a fairly handsome fellow, plus without the glasses, he was mostly just biceps, and chiselled jawline and…. She shook her head. That was simply unprofessional. She was advisor to the president and on a mission and it was inappropriate, most likely, somehow. She wasn't paid, so technically she could...no, no, no, she thought. She dashed all thoughts of handsome guards from her mind. They finally had a suspect, and it was time to find this key of Impasto and bring this caper to a close.

CHAPTER NINETEEN

"Who are you working for?"

"Nobody, I'm senator Zwart. I work for the people."

"We know that much. Why did you steal the key?"

"I did not!"

"Why was it found in your home then?" Cassidy asked.

"That is impossible."

"Really? Well, here it is. And it was found in your home just this morning. We received an anonymous tip that it was there and so we sent detectives and sure enough." President Corie held up the oblong object, no bigger than a small water glass that presumably held the data of the country inside it.

"Therefore, you are under arrest for theft of the key of Impasto, treason, resisting arrest, and will be brought to a grey room to wait out your trial which shouldn't take more than six months to complete."

"But I didn't take it…"

"We found it in your house."

"It shouldn't have been there."

"Well, that's odd, because it was." Cassidy walked

around him. "So if you didn't take it—"

"It was found in his house—" Raph said.

"Are you saying it was planted there?" Cassidy carried on. She stood back, one finger on her chin.

"I — didn't say that."

"What's the sentence for treason and theft of the key?" Cassidy asked President Corie.

"Life in the grey room. No chance of parole."

"What about for having knowledge of the crime but not actually being the thief, President?" Cassidy asked.

"Oh, if a person had knowledge, they'd get at least fifteen years. Unless, of course…"

"What?" Cassidy watched the prisoner's face.

"Obviously whoever stole it didn't care about you or the country and now they've given up, returned the key to President Corie, and will likely go unpunished while you languish in the grey room," Raph said.

"Well, I say let's just throw him in the grey room anyway. All this talk of setting him up is just a ploy. We have the key, it was in his house, he is guilty. His poor family. The shame they'll face. And losing their home. They can't stay in a senatorial residence."

"See to their removal," President Corie ordered.

The guard, Micho, made movement towards the door as though to follow orders.

"Okay, okay. I'll tell you. It was Mayor Gades of Saged who did it. He was so angry. He thinks you'll implement the pretty prisons and abolish the grey and that you should not have won. He has the contract to run the grey prisons, you know. He stole the key but when it didn't help him win the election, he decided to use it to frame

President Corie which sent his supporters after her. She was truly in grave danger before she left. So, it was good she left, but that's when he wrote the letter. To frame you for it so that he could take over. But that stubborn Eryn refused to allow it and stood as acting president and then he didn't know what to do. He's a terrible president. I guess Gades decided to plant it on me to make you stop looking at him."

"So where was the key this entire time? Before it was planted on you?"

"Right under your nose," Senator Zwart said. Then told them precisely where it was hidden. Both Cassidy and Corie gasped when he said the name of the place.

CHAPTER TWENTY

The Lamartine Cottage was as picturesque as Cassidy recalled. She entered and walked towards the kitchen. Raph and Micho followed her, and she nodded to the cabinet above the stove. They reached in with their gloved hands and pulled it open and took out a biscuit tin. Inside, nestled in a bed of velvet was the key of Impasto.

"It's the real one this time?" President Corie inquired from the doorway.

"It is, indeed."

"I can't believe we stayed here, and it was right there all along."

"Gades was clever. He decided to hide it here. If it were ever found, Corie would be blamed.

"And you got his full confession on tape?"

"Thanks to Senator Zwart."

"What will happen to Zwart?"

"We gave him immunity for his testimony. I will let him remain a senator. He did do wrong, but he helped us find the key."

"I can't believe he didn't question the fake key."

"He knew it was being used to frame you, so it wasn't

hard for him to imagine that he was the victim being framed. Plus, he's not the brightest hue in the palette," Corie replied.

"Well, that's it then. Is this place under police protection as a crime scene now?" Cassidy asked. "I'd love to stay here for a little while, have a vacation, before I return to—" she glanced at the guards, "home."

Micho raised an eyebrow, then turned quickly to follow Raph.

"You must use it. You are very welcome to stay, Cassidy. You helped find the key. It was your plan that created a confession. Please, stay here as long as you want and when you are ready I will send Micho to find you and escort you back home."

She still only trusted him and Raph with Cassidy's origins.

"Cassidy Cane, thank you for all you have done." Eryn walked into the cottage.

"Eryn!" Corie greeted him with enthusiasm.

"So, you're friends again?" Cassidy asked.

"Yes, we are." Eryn replied. He smiled and Corie met his eyes.

"I'm glad to hear it."

"Please, everyone leave. I must speak to Cassidy Cane alone." Corie waved them all out.

Soon the room was empty, and the President of Impasto and Cassidy walked alone to sit. Corie poured herself a liberal glass of absinthe.

"We have been on an adventure, my friend," Corie said.

"Indeed, we have," Cassidy replied.

"I have a gift for you. It is not much. A token really." Corie pulled a small box out of her pocket and handed it to Cassidy.

She untied the pretty ribbon and flipped open the box. There lay a pendant the size of a silver dollar. She brought it up close and smiled. It contained a tiny window that looked somewhat familiar.

"I should only look at this with the glasses on, I suspect." She wasn't much for baubles but it was pretty and a lovely souvenir.

"Yes, indeed. I know you're not a jewelry person, but I want you to think beyond that. It might be a useful tool to add you your bag. If it entrances you, perhaps it entrances some of the others you might encounter on your adventures who might not be so friendly as my people are."

"This is a wonderful gift! Thank you!" Cassidy said. This could have a very practical purpose aside from being remarkably beautiful. And here she was thinking this was one adventure from which she wouldn't be bringing an artifact back.

"I've been thinking, your world is very beautiful, but it has its troubles and its darkness. You can't always hide all that behind enchanting beauty," Cassidy said. "Be careful there."

Corie considered her words for a moment, then spoke. "But Cassidy Cane, you've made an error. The beauty of our world wasn't created to hide the pain. It was created from pain. It is art and isn't that what art is supposed to do? Takes the agony of the artist and their lived experience and make something beautiful from them? We just nurture this to a greater degree, as a priority. That is all.

We know there is pain but from that we draw exquisite beauty. Perhaps our world has more because we have had more pain, not less. Either way, it's a pleasure to live in it. And I will forever be grateful you brought me home. I must go. Duty calls. The *real* key must be placed in a safe location and I must deal with senator Zwart. You see I want his vote on a matter that was held up before I left. If he agrees to vote with me, I will be very successful in my first big decision as president."

"Good luck President Corie," Cassidy said.

"Good luck to you as well. Cassidy Cane."

CHAPTER TWENTY-ONE

Cassidy leaned back, remembering all she had seen at the labs Corie had arranged for her to tour before leaving. The most magnificent being the display of snow globes where big things lived in small worlds. Animals frolicking safely in conservation areas where nobody could hunt them and fields growing food that no pest or storm could destroy. These people were mad, beautiful geniuses.

Things were so different in a world where imagination and visual art led the way. She'd been given an entire library of movies and television shows, so well-scripted and performed by Corie's people, a person felt incredibly immersed in the program. Not entranced like when she went outside without her sunglasses, but close.

She had only noticed one thing missing in their world and when she'd mentioned it to the scientists, they'd gone off in a frenzy thinking about it. Cassidy had noticed that for all the magnificent things in their world, they did not have birds or bats or insects. Pollination happened with just the wind. So it went that they also did not have any flying objects except for the ability of their road machines, under the right conditions, to elevate for short periods of time.

Upon mentioning this oddity, and telling how in her world people travelled by plane regularly and that birds sang beautiful songs and flew like they floated in the air, they'd immediately started designing an airplane-like vehicle that played beautiful music and contained small libraries, and was decorated with beautiful art. The fact that they didn't yet know how to make things fly seemed not to bother them much. It would come. She also warned them that planes caused pollution problems in their world and to design their flying machines to run clean so as not to destroy their air. Corie, now president, had written a legislative bill immediately on that very topic, so there was no risk of their newest technology causing any trouble in that way. "Means only justifies the end if the means causes no harm," She'd wisely said before reading the bill in her parliament.

"So strange," Cassidy said, remembering all that.

"What?" Professor Gamgee inquired from his seat beside her.

"I'll tell you all about it when we get home."

"So, she really is going to change all the grey prison rooms to those pretty worlds?" Professor Gamgee asked.

"She is. Senator Zwart gave the deciding vote as payment to make up for aligning against President Corie. She's got a big imagination but she's a heck of a dealmaker too. Ironically the first prisoner to occupy one is Mayor Gades who was found guilty of stealing the key of Impasto. Quite fitting, given he stole the key and tried to sabotage her presidency in the first place due to his objections to Corie's idea about prison reform."

"Marvelous. Simply marvelous."

"Yes, it is." But he wasn't listening to her anymore. Instead he was reading a letter.

"What is it?" Cassidy asked, glancing at the paper in his hand and recognizing the tone of Dr. Gamgee's voice. Something was up.

"Well, there's this situation brewing that is highly important, you won't believe it when I tell you!" He waved the letter around. "It is the most spectacular thing. I really can't believe it myself."

"Tell me then." Cassidy looked at him with anticipation. Was it another adventure for her? A massive funding grant for his research? A sale on his favourite pens?

Dr. Herbert Gambee opened his mouth, then snapped it shut again. He looked all round the plane that was now full of passengers and shook his head.

"What? After all that buildup you're not going to tell me? You can't just do that!" Cassidy crossed her arms and formed her lips into a pout.

"I'm sorry, Cassidy. Not here, not now. It's much too crowded. You're just going to have to wait until we land to find out." He folded up the letter and put it away.

"Fine, but once we land you better tell me quickly," she said. "You know I simply *hate* waiting."

COMING SOON!
THE FRANKLIN EXPEDITION
BY JD RYOT & PAUL CARBERRY!

Cassidy Cane goes by many titles -- archeologist, anthropologist, adventurer -- but none more fitting than that given to her on some strange worlds: Slipstreamer.

Cassidy slips between worlds, traveling to bizarre planets and alternate Earths to find extraordinary new technologies and artifacts that might better humanity!

On a trip to a time-displaced frozen tundra, Cassidy must defeat the Tuurngait, a polar creature of myth and legend that guards an impossible disc with the power to run cities on clean energy for generations. Limited by the technology of this world trapped in the year 1845, can she save herself and the Peglars from the beast?

Coauthored with international bestseller Paul Carberry!
Not to be missed!

ACKNOWLEDGEMENTS

The authors would like to pay special thanks to the *Slipstreamers* committee at Engen Books, including Amanda Labonté, Matthew LeDrew, Ali House, Ellen Curtis, Erin Vance, and, Lauralana Dunne.

Without their tireless efforts, none of this would have been possible.

Special thanks to this episode's editor, AJ Ryan.

Carolyn R Parsons would also like to thank Dante Fuller, her favourite adventurer in this world.

ABOUT THE AUTHOR

Carolyn R. Parsons is a full-time writer and radio personality residing in Lewisporte, NL. She has contributed to *The Central Voice*, the Saltire network of papers, and *Downhome Magazine*. Her books include a poetry collection, two novels and a collection of short stories. Her 2017 novel, Charley through Canada, attained bestseller status on Amazon.

Parsons is on the Board of the Writers Alliance of Newfoundland and Labrador (WANL) as the representative for Central/Burin. She was a contributor to 2018's bestselling photography book, *Kit Sora: The Artobiography*, with her flash fiction: 'The Doorway Home.'

Her most recent novel, *The Forbidden Dreams of Betsy Elliott*, was released in February 2019.

JD Ryot is the reclusive creator of the *Slipstreamers* series from Engen Books. JD is an avid fan of young adult literature and adventure serials. When asked if they had come to this world through a portal themselves, JD Ryot refused to answer. No record of their birth has ever been found... on this world.